OPERA OBSCURA

OPERA OBSCURA

A WHOLLY IMPROBABLE SELECTION OF IMPOSSIBLE OPERA

written and illustrated by
PETER KENT

RENARD PRESS

RENARD PRESS LTD

124 City Road
London EC1V 2NX
United Kingdom
info@renardpress.com
020 8050 2928

www.renardpress.com

Opera Obscura first published by Renard Press Ltd in 2022

Text and illustrations © Peter Kent, 2022

Cover illustrations by Peter Kent
Cover and type design by Will Dady

Printed in the United Kingdom by Severn

ISBN: 978-1-80447-013-8

9 8 7 6 5 4 3 2 1

Peter Kent asserts his moral right to be identified as the author of this work in accordance with the Copyright, Designs and Patents Act 1988.

This is a work of fiction. As a volume of parody pieces, many of the statements that purport to be facts are actually fiction.

Renard Press is proud to be a climate positive publisher, removing more carbon from the air than we emit and planting a small forest. For more information see renardpress.com/eco.

All rights reserved. This publication may not be reproduced, stored in a retrieval system or transmitted, in any form or by any means – electronic, mechanical, photocopying, recording or otherwise – without the prior permission of the publisher.

CONTENTS

OPERA OBSCURA	9
Introduction	11
HAUNGDI DE HEXIE YU TIAN GUO ZHI QUAN	12
(*The Emperor's Harmonious and Heavenly Fist*)	
EL LIBRO DE MODALES	14
(*The Book of Manners*)	
DE VLOEK VAN TULPEN	16
(*The Curse of the Tulips*)	
SVIN'YA S NOSOM NA ZOLOTO	18
(*The Pig With a Nose for Gold*)	
LA TEMPESTA	20
(*The Tempest*)	
IL SCOCCIATORE BIGOTTO	22
(*The Sanctimonious Pest*)	
ACHILLEIOS PTERNA	24
(*The Heel of Achilles*)	
DAS AUSGEFRANSTE SEIL	26
(*The Frayed Rope*)	
O FEIJÃO DOURADO DA MORTE	28
(*The Golden Bean of Death*)	
* ***************	30
(*The Lucky Card*)	
LA MARMITE VIDE	32
(*The Empty Casserole*)	
TEKI NI CHIKADZUKU	34
(*Closer to the Enemy*)	

AABHAAREE HO	36
(Count Your Blessings)	
KRAKEN	38
(The Kraken)	
MALLEUS HAERETICORUM	40
(The Hammer of the Heretics)	
OBŘÍ KAPR	42
(The Enormous Carp)	
GIGANTSKAYA KURSKAYA GUSENITSA	44
(The Giant Caterpillar of Kursk)	
THE WALSINGHAM WAY	46
DER FLIEGENDE HAMBURGER	48
(The Flying Hamburger)	
THE ROUGH AND THE FAIR	50
LONG, LONG TRAIN O' MISERY	52
OPERA ANTARCTICA	54
(Antarctic Opera)	
ÄR VI DÄR ÄN?	56
(Are We There Yet?)	
THE FATAL COMPACT	58
x(0=z2x; <1000.0)<x=o/c2>	60
(Reach for the Stars)	
Incredible Opera Houses	62
Incredible Instruments	74
A Selective Glossary	77

OPERA OBSCURA

INTRODUCTION

DOCTOR JOHNSON WAS RIGHT when he described opera as 'an exotic and irrational entertainment', although he could have added 'always expensive and often excruciating'. The very first opera was called *Dafne*, written in Italy by Jacopo Peri in 1598, with a libretto by Ottavio Rinuccini. Since then well over ten thousand operas have been written and performed – that's over a thousand days, about three years, of continuous music and drama. These, however, are only the works that have been brought to life on the stage. There are thousands more that have never been performed and remain, like Frankenstein's monster, inert, awaiting the enlivening spark. Of those that have been produced, very few remain in the repertoire today. Only about a hundred operas receive regular professional performances, while two hundred or so pass in and out of fashion, but never quite out of mind. Another four hundred are revived at minor opera festivals or performed at music colleges. The rest are forgotten, languishing in manuscript form or lost, either completely or as ghosts half living on in snatches of other music. Clever, ambitious young conductors, forced down ever more obscure musical paths to gain attention, often blow the dust off some long-forgotten piece and bring it back to life in a stripped-down performance with a tiny cast and orchestra. Some of these rarities are briefly acclaimed, but in most cases the praise is due to the effort involved in their exhumation rather than any enjoyment of the work itself. Afterwards the revived opera, like an old person briefly reawoken by bright young things, usually returns to the obscurity it deserves.

This book contributes a small number to that shadowy horde, giving a brief synopsis of banal and bizarre plots so obscure they could almost be true, and a short account of the disastrous productions that could have denied them their chance of ever being established in the repertoire. It is safe to predict that none will ever make it to the stage, and they will be for ever Opera Obscura.

PETER KENT
2022

HAUNGDI DE HEXIE YU TIAN GUO ZHI QUAN

(The Emperor's Harmonious and Heavenly Fist)

China, 1250

CHINESE OPERA HAS NEVER appealed to western ears. 'A hideous concatenation of the most excruciating aural combinations,' complained the eminent musicologist Charles Burney,[1] and he had heard only the more bland and tuneful examples of the genre that had started to become popular in London. The most mysterious and revered of all works was the *Imperial Dragon Opera*, which was performed on auspicious occasions, and in the presence only of the Emperor and his deaf eunuchs in the Jade Opera House within the Forbidden City. *The Emperor's Harmonious and Heavenly Fist*, to give its full title, was composed by the eminent courtier and musician Xingming during – ironically – the Song Dynasty, in about 1250. Reports of the contents are vague; it is unlikely that anyone has ever known it in its complete form. It is said to have involved dragons, labyrinths, the ghosts of emperors, the souls of two lovers turned into cormorants and much celestial conjuring. The music was scored for an enlarged Chinese orchestra of plucked instruments and variegated percussion, but with the addition of a water-powered organ and two great bronze horns said to be over thirty feet long.

So rare were performances there was only one during the eighteenth century. This was given in 1794 to the British mission of Lord George Macartney as an extraordinary mark of favour. Warned of what to expect, the diplomats plugged their ears with chewed mulberry leaves. Unfortunately, the Scottish scientist James Dinwiddie stuffed his ears with opium paste, which he ingested by diffusion. His consequent hallucinations during a particularly solemn part of the performance brought an abrupt ending to all negotiations and the expulsion of the mission.

The bulk of the manuscript and costumes were lost when the Summer Palace was destroyed and looted by the British in 1860,[2] and the remainder was finished off by the Red Guards during the Cultural Revolution. 'Let us crush with our heroic proletarian feet the reactionary harmonies of the *Emperor's Fist*,' proclaimed Chairman Mao.

---

1 An English organist, minor composer and author of the four-volume *A General History of Music* (1776–89), Charles Burney was the father of two novelists – Fanny and Sarah Burney – as well as three other children, including a future priest and scholar, also called Charles, who was sent down from Cambridge for stealing books. He had wit and erudition and a strong dislike of French music.

2 This happened at the end of the 1860 Opium War. British peace envoys were tortured and killed by the Chinese and, in revenge, the sumptuous Summer Palace was looted and burned. Amongst the booty taken was a Pekinese dog, the first to be seen in England. It was given to Queen Victoria and untactfully christened Looty.

HAUNGDI DE HEXIE YU TIAN GUO ZHI QUAN

In October 2003, when the *Antiques Roadshow* visited Dumfries Ice Bowl, a very large porcelain plate with a scene from the opera was brought by a descendant of James Dinwiddie. It caused great excitement amongst the experts and was valued at £80,000. After the usual token protestations that it would never leave the family, it was sent to Christies' and sold for nearly twice that amount to a semiconductor magnate from Shenzhen. It is thought to represent one of the fourteen forbidden scenes, but, as to what is actually happening, nobody has the slightest idea.

EL LIBRO DE MODALES

(The Book of Manners)

Spain, 1647

When one imagines Spanish music one thinks of passionate guitars, castanets and foot-stamping sultriness, so it is surprising to learn that a Spanish opera is distinguished as one of the dullest, dreariest and most unloved of all time. A work so excruciatingly, numbingly boring that the Inquisition was petitioned to ban it on the grounds that it would tempt souls to commit the unforgivable sin of despairing suicide.

Opera was slow to develop in Spain compared with France and Italy, which had a continuous tradition of opera from the early seventeenth century. In Spain, however, the preference was for spoken drama, and critics asserted that opera was a less worthy art form. At the time morbidly religious and rigidly hieratic, Spain viewed opera as an indulgent frippery bordering on heresy.

To prove the critics and the Inquisition wrong, the composer Juan Hidalgo de Polanco and the writer Lope de Vega collaborated to write *El libro de modales*. It was the usual comedy of manners: a confection of a pert, pretty minx, a besotted old fool, a handsome rogue and an assortment of comic servants. The first draft was a genuinely witty satire, but it soon fell so foul of political and religious censorship that it ended up as a kind of dramatised court etiquette manual. Objections to the amount of music, combined with de Polanco's extreme slowness in composition[1] and great difficulty in setting words, resulted in an opera with hardly any singing at all. Mostly it consisted of dancing and musical fencing. This pleased nobody except the stone-deaf Philip IV, a great swordsman in his youth. After his death in 1665 *El libro de modales* was never performed again. The manuscript is still in the library of the Escorial, where it is occasionally examined by visiting scholars – but never for long.

---

[1] Rossini was said to be able to write a whole opera in a week. De Polanco once managed an aria in a month. His most substantial work, a cavatina for viola, would have been longer had the ink on the manuscript not faded before he had finished it.

In this scene the Count of Miranda del Castañar – old and ugly but extremely rich – and the Marquess of Chinchilla – poor and palsied, but of impeccable and ancient lineage – dance a stately pavane in a contest to win the hand of Maria Infanta. She stands on the balcony of the palace of her scheming guardian. Don Pedro Ximenez, the handsome rogue, edges towards her disguised as a statue of El Cid. So much money had been spent on the lavish costumes of the principals that the chorus were economically clad in the robes of penitents. The rhythm of the pavane was cleverly amplified by the clank of armour and the regular clink of penitential chains.

DE VLOEK VAN TULPEN

(The Curse of the Tulips)

The Netherlands, 1785

There is only one occasion when the audience of an opera has literally been swept off its feet on the opening night – although at the premiere of *The Curse of the Tulips*, it was not by enthusiasm but a flood of cold water. The Netherlands has never developed a national school of opera; audiences have historically shunned the home-grown and shown a preference for Italian, French and German works. On rare occasions Dutch composers have risen to the challenge, but have inevitably failed.[1]

In 1784 the burghers of Bergen op Zoom committed money to build an opera house, and they patriotically decided that their new theatre must be opened with a new Dutch opera. *De vloek van tulpen* was composed for the occasion by T.C.P. Bach[2] (the Dutch Bach), with a libretto by Jacobus Leyden Jarr (polymath and inventor of a saucepan for poaching eggs). The four-act opera, set in the late sixteenth century[3] during the reign of William the Silent – who has a very big part sung by a baritone – relates the sorry saga of a noble family who lose all their money in tulip speculation. To restore their fortune and to save his sister from being forced to marry a villainous dwarf, the hero, Gert van Gouda, sells secrets to Philip II of Spain.

Sentenced to death, only the pleas of his fiancée save Gert, and he is doomed to sail the seas for ever in a seven-masted ship with black sails and a crew of fire-breathing dogs. However, while being blown about the North Sea, he helps Sir Francis Drake defeat the Spanish Armada and is allowed to return for one day to marry his sweetheart. As soon as he sets foot on Dutch soil, the golden tulip that ruined him blooms, the evil dwarf is pinioned to the sails of a windmill, the Spanish army flees, the town bell – also known as William the Silent, as it has not tolled for fifty years – peals and his bride arrives at the church. Then, suddenly, as is the way in opera, she dies.

As the curtain came down on the opening night to moderate applause, the dyke holding back the North Sea broke – the burghers had diverted the funds for repairing the sea defences to the opera house – and the deluge drowned the prospects of Dutch vernacular opera. Fortunately, few of the audience perished; most managed to clamber aboard the seven-masted ship, whilst T.C.P. Bach paddled to safety on a double bass.

---

1 The one notable exception is the 1834 Dutch-language opera *Saffo* by Johannes Bernardus van Bree. However, it is not popular anywhere else.
2 He was a cousin of C.P.E. Bach (the English Bach), N.H.S. Bach (the Polish Bach), B.B.C. Bach (the Alsatian Bach), U.S.A. Bach (the Irish Bach) and J.C.B. Bach (the American Bach).
3 Polymath he may have been, but he was ignorant of history. The tulip mania did not occur until the 1630s, fifty years after the opera is set.

Death scenes are normally prolonged in opera, but the length of scene in which Anna (Gert's fiancée) dies and is mourned stretched endurance to the limit. Wilhelmina van Veen, playing Anna, lay so long on the cold stage she caught a chill and ruined the illusion with a prolonged fit of sneezing.

SVIN'YA S NOSOM NA ZOLOTO

(The Pig With a Nose for Gold)

Russia, 1705

WHILE IT IS GENERALLY AGREED that the performance and production of opera has greatly improved, it is also true that the sartorial standards of the audience have declined. White ties, tiaras and glittering gowns are rarely seen these days: audiences now opt for comfort. Nobody today would advocate the style police enforcing a stricter dress code – but this actually did happen in eighteenth-century Russia. The results were calamitous – both for the audience and the opera.

Opera was introduced to Russia by Peter the Great. In love with everything modern the West had to offer, he made an extended visit to Holland and England, where he learned shipbuilding, locksmithing and tried his hand at dentistry. While in Holland he first heard an opera staged by an Italian company and fell in love with its drama and melody. Russian music then consisted only of the ponderous solemnities of Orthodox religious chant and a type of extremely primitive song: the three-part homorhythmic Russian *kant*.

One of the first buildings erected in Peter's new city of St Petersburg was an opera house, and a new work was commissioned to inaugurate it. *The Pig with a Nose for Gold* was an adaption of a Russian folk tale with a libretto by William Sheepspear[1] and music by Domenico Caldara, who was alarmed to find that the climate, cuisine and urban amenities were nothing like those promised to lure him from Naples.

A peasant girl, Anya, has a pig, Ludmilla. Although useless at rooting for truffles she has – like a porcine metal detector – an infallible nose for finding buried gold. This makes Anya very rich. The evil King of Sweden seeks her hand – and pig – in marriage, while a wicked band of Prussian knights, a coven of witches and a synod of reactionary clergy all plot to kidnap the pig.

There is a happy ending, when the handsome young Tsar of Muscovy defeats the Swedes, knights, witches and clergy and marries Anya. Ludmilla's treasure-hunting nose is put to good use enriching and empowering Mother Russia.

The first night of the opera was a disaster. To make Russia look modern, the Tsar had announced a decree banning the long beards and trailing sleeves worn by nobles. Peter himself stood in the foyer and forcibly shaved the beards and snipped the sleeves of all those who defied him. This, combined with the Tsar's mischievous insistence that a chorus of swine who persecute Ludmilla be sung by Orthodox bishops and abbots, caused a riot, which was eventually suppressed with enthusiastic brutality. After the opera house burned down, half the audience had been drowned in the River Neva and the rest deported to Siberia, Peter turned his attention to casting cannon and clockmaking, and opera was heard no more.

---

1 William Sheepspear was an English fur merchant living in Russia. The Tsar was convinced he had written *Hamlet* and *King Lear*, and Sheepspear thought it prudent not to correct the misapprehension.

SVIN'YA S NOSOM NA ZOLOTO

In this scene, Ludmilla the pig – played by a boy soprano kidnapped in Dresden and smuggled to Russia in a sack of potatoes – is threatened by the evil witch, Baba Yaga. The witch's hut, traditionally on bird's legs, is here on wheels, as the Tsar thought them more modern. Behind the hut a chorus of Prussian knights sing of their secret intention to roast the pig and steal the gold. The Archbishop of Novgorod and his trio of holy pigs, with noses that sniff out heresy, are about to condemn Ludmilla and Anya for sorcery and have them burned but not eaten. Some of the audience were so enraged by this blasphemy that they stormed the stage. This set off the general riot which ended in the destruction of the opera house.

LA TEMPESTA[1]

(The Tempest)

Somewhere in the South Atlantic, 1740

THE SEA IS A VAST, turbulent stage of tragedy, and nautical calamities have inspired many great works of art, not least Géricault's *The Raft of the Medusa* and Samuel James Arnold's comic opera *The Shipwreck*, staged in 1796 at Drury Lane. Arnold was – and historians of opera still are – unaware that this was preceded by a unique work, staged on a desert island fifty years before.

In 1739 the sixth-rate HMS *Phoenix*, commanded by Captain Edward Baker, was ordered to sail to Jamaica to test two rival methods of navigation. On board were Gideon Dawkins, the blind watchmaker of Oxford, with his marine chronometer, and the Reverend Rumsby Wells, an advocate of the Lunar Distance Method. Unfortunately the *Phoenix*, due to errors of calculation and an inaccurate clock, grounded in the shallows of a small uncharted island just off northern Brazil. There was just time to get the crew and some stores ashore before the ship broke up and sank.

As the island had an ideal climate, no work was necessary to survive, and the men soon became bored and fractious. Captain Baker set them to digging holes all over the island, but when they failed to unearth any buried treasure, he feared mutiny. The captain suggested that Reverend Wells staged an opera to keep the men busy and entertained. Dawkins wrote, or rather dictated, the libretto (basically *The Tempest* in simple rhyming couplets) and Wells, a competent organist, devised the music.

Instruments were a problem – only the ship's bell, the bosun's whistle, an accordion and a couple of fiddles had survived the wreck. But Dawkins and the ship's carpenters, with wondrous dexterity, soon contrived a small ensemble of makeshift instruments. The giant bamboo that grew profusely on the island provided the pipes for a small organ, bassoons, flutes and clarinets. Conches of various sizes substituted for a brass section. Viols and cellos were fashioned from gourds and turtle shells strung with sisal, and an ingenious set of percussion instruments were created from logs and coconuts.

After months of happy activity the opera was staged on an idyllic terrace overlooking the sparkling sea. At the end, as Prospero grants Ariel his freedom and prepares to leave the island, a cannon was heard, and cast and audience looked out to see HMS *Kent* dropping anchor.

Only the audience of the Royal Opera House rushing for the last train to Bexley have been known to move faster than the sailors as they rushed down the beach towards freedom. It transpired that the *Kent* was also testing the Dawkins chronometer, which proves that, even if spectacularly inaccurate, it was at least consistent. Because of the navigational errors, no one is certain exactly where this unique performance of a castaway opera performed by castaways actually took place, and the sole record of its existence is in the log book of the *Phoenix*, which is held in The National Archives.

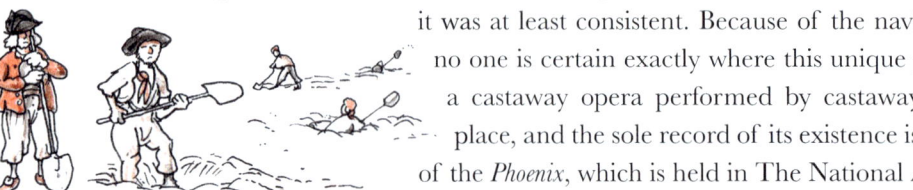

---

1 The libretto was, of course, in English, but Wells decided that convention demanded an Italian title.

LA TEMPESTA

La Tempesta is one of only three operas to have an all-male cast: Rachmaninoff's *The Miserly Knight* and Britten's *Billy Budd* are the other two. In this final scene, Prospero was played by the ship's master-at-arms, who had a fine baritone with excellent projection, honed by years of bellowing at sailors. Beside him, as a symbol of his dominion over space and time, is Dawkins' useless chronometer. Ariel, in feather costume, awaits his release, while Caliban crouches scowling. In the background HMS *Kent* approaches the island, while in the foliage above the stage an audience of silent monkeys watches with interest. As the *Kent*'s navigational equipment was as useless as the *Phoenix*'s, the exact location of the island remains a mystery. However, in 1955 Hans and Lotte Hass visited an uninhabited island in the Saint Peter and Saint Paul Archipelago, where they were intrigued by the large number of crater-like depressions, which they thought were turtle nests. Also of interest were the calls of the monkeys, which were surprisingly tuneful, and often in harmony.

IL SCOCCIATORE BIGOTTO

(The Sanctimonious Pest)

Italy, 1814

MOST FORGOTTEN OPERAS DESERVE their fate, but occasionally a work is the victim of unjust circumstance. Such a piece is *Il scocciatore bigotto*, a charming opera buffa by Eliodoro Pestano, who wrote the score in three weeks to a libretto by Gaetano Caproni. The opera is set in a bucolic Umbrian town where the Bigotte – a band of pious old maids – petition the bishop to remove their affable and easy-going priest. His replacement is the austere and incorruptible Don Succhiotto.

In scenes moving from farce to religious fervour, the new priest reimposes the Church's authority. The first act, which closes with Don Succhiotto drilling a squad of altar boys and the town militia while trying to stop the hunting guild's annual pigeon shoot on the church roof, is pure madcap delight.

In the second act Don Succhiotto is subjected to, and resists, every sensual and spiritual temptation. The townsfolk despair – even the Bigotte turn against him – but they eventually accept he cannot be changed. Then, at a fiesta, the image of Jesus slips from the arms of the Madonna to crash on the priest's head.

Don Succhiotto lies in a coma while the townsfolk pray. They vow to reform should he, against all expectation, live. (There is a delightful, encyclopaedic patter song, '*Non c'e speranza*',[1] sung as the doctor lists all his symptoms.) Then, a miracle happens: Don Succhiotto rises, completely cured, from his sickbed to announce that tolerance of human frailty is the true message of the gospels, not rigid obedience to ecclesiastical law. The fountain runs with wine and the hunting guild fires a fusillade to a chorus of ecstatic celebration.

At the time of the first performance the liberal Roman Republic had given way to the reactionary rule of the Pope. The opera was banned and the manuscript burned by the public executioner. Pestano fled to Turin, where he gave up music for politics.[2] Fragments of the music survive, borrowed by Rossini for several of his later operas.

---

1 'There is no hope'.
2 Prominent in the Italian Nationalist movement, he was deputy minister for telegraphs in the first government of the united Italy.

IL SCOCCIATORE BIGOTTO

In this scene, 'The Three Graces', Adina, Bettina and Cantina seek to embarrass Don Succhiotto by claiming he is wearing Adina's nightdress. This, more than anything else, enraged the papal censor.

ACHILLEIOS PTERNA

(The Heel of Achilles)

Greece, 1823

EXHAUSTED AND AILING from the effects of sexual excess Lord Byron, philhellene, poet and libertine visited Corfu[1] in 1823 to recuperate. The least glamorous of his many afflictions were painful corns and flat feet. While resting he amused himself by writing a libretto inspired by reading a chiropodist's manual and an erotic novel, *The Secrets of the Sultan's Seraglio*.

The resulting opera, *The Heel of Achilles*, was a comedy set during the first great siege of Corfu by the Turks in 1537. The hero, a Greek patriot named Metatarsus, and his companions, Tarlus and Caleomus, disguise themselves as eunuchs to infiltrate the harem of the Turkish Sultan, Suleiman the Sumptuous, in an attempt to rescue the Venetian princess, Constanza di Hyperbole. Suleiman's Achilles' heel is his Armenian cook, who alone can provide the voluptuous Turkish delight his master craves. Metatarsus seduces the cook (a trouser role scored for a contralto or castrato), and in return for the restoration of his culinary services, Suleiman agrees to release the princess and raise the siege.

The music, composed by the founder of the Ionian school, Nikolaos Mantzaros, was a witty and tuneful fusion of Italian buffa and demotic Greek elements. The libretto was translated into Greek – rather inaccurately – by the poet Dionysios Solomos, who claimed *The Hymn to Liberty* (later to become the Greek National Anthem) as his own.

All was set for a triumphant first performance at the Nobile Teatro but, alas, Byron's flagrant priapic activity, despite his corns, outraged the Lord High Commissioner Sir Thomas Maitland, whose wife, daughter and aide de camp the poet had debauched.

On the evening of the performance Sir Thomas ordered a three-hour practice of the garrison artillery, accompanied by massed regimental bands in the square outside the theatre. Hardly a note of the opera could be heard against the thunderous cacophony of cannon and brass bands. Disgusted, Byron left for mainland Greece to join the fight for independence, and died of fever at Missolonghi the following year. The score of the opera and Byron's manuscript were preserved in the Teatro until they were lost when Corfu was bombed by the Luftwaffe in 1943.

---

1 Formerly ruled by Venice, Corfu became a British protectorate in 1815, governed by an official with a title straight from Gilbert and Sullivan: The Lord High Commissioner of the Ionian Isles. British control lasted until 1864 when Corfu was united to Greece.

Byron cherished a desire to have sexual relations in the basket of a balloon while flying over the English Channel. He would have fulfilled it had not the pioneer female aeronaut and focus of his erotic fascination, Sophie Blanchard, perished in a pyrotechnic spectacular.[1] Frustrated, his hopes dashed, Byron wrote a lengthy scene where the hero and heroine escape in a balloon from Suleiman, who has reneged on his deal. Here we see the basket ascending with Metatarsus and Constanza while the Sultan, exhausted by the attentions of his odalisques and bloated with Turkish delight, sinks into a stupor.

---

1 Sophie Blanchard was the first female aeronaut, a pioneering balloonist famed and feted throughout Europe. She was the first woman to make a solo flight, and it is thought that Napoleon appointed her Chief Air Minister of Ballooning, a role in which she designed plans for an aerial invasion of England. In 1819 she achieved the macabre distinction of being the first woman to be killed in an aviation accident. During a flight from the Tivoli Gardens in Paris she set off fireworks that, not surprisingly, ignited the gas in her balloon. Her craft crashed on the roof of a house and she fell to her death in the street below.

DAS AUSGEFRANSTE SEIL

(The Frayed Rope)

Switzerland, 1867

ONE WOULD NOT THINK that an opera about four men tumbling to a terrible death on jagged rocks to the accompaniment of alpine horns and despairing yodels would be a success – and one would be right. The rare Swiss opera *The Frayed Rope* is the retelling of the first ascent of the Matterhorn and the fatal accident on the descent that tainted the triumph with tragedy. On the 14th of July 1865 Edward Whymper, three fellow Englishmen and two Swiss guides were the first climbers to reach the summit of the last unconquered alpine peak. On the way down four lost their footing and fell;[1] the rope stretching between Whymper and the guide, Peter Taugwalder, and the unfortunate four broke, and they slid over a precipice to their doom.

The macabre drama shocked and fascinated all Europe, and it was not long before the Swiss composer Joachim Raff began work on an opera on the theme. His librettist was the playwright Gottfried Keller, and the finished work received its premiere at Basel in 1869. Musically it was grand and expressive, an early forerunner of Strauss' *Alpine Symphony*, but it was hated by the English.

All England revered Whymper's fallen companions as martyrs to the new sport of mountaineering, and regarded the opera as a frivolous slur on noble athletes. Queen Victoria wrote to all her numerous German relations asking that they put pressure on the Swiss to ban it.[2] She took particular exception to the copious amounts of cowbells, yodelling and the series of diminishing bouncing chords accompanying the fatal fall. Most of the nation (but not all) were outraged by the suggestion that Lord Francis Douglas, whose body was never found, had seduced an innocent milkmaid whose outraged father, the guide Peter Taugwalder, had cut the safety rope to avenge his daughter's honour.[3] English tourists were essential to the mountain economy of Switzerland; the opera was withdrawn and soon forgotten.

---

1 They were Charles Hudson, Lord Francis Douglas, Douglas Hadow and Michael Croz. Lord Francis was the uncle of the infamous 'Bosie', the ruin of Oscar Wilde.
2 *The News Chronicle* went further in its demands that this slur on British courage be avenged. 'A gunboat must be dispatched at once to bring this nation of cheesemongers and slanderers to heel!' its editorial thundered, until the geographical impossibility of this was regretfully acknowledged.
3 There were dark rumours that the connection between Lord Francis and Whymper was more than the hemp cord, and that Whymper might have every reason to sever it.

When the doomed four slid to their deaths over the precipice, singing continually, it was necessary that they faced the audience. A thick cloud was generated from dry ice just before their fall that provided cover for mattresses to be brought out for the singers' landing. This did not always work as planned. At one performance the mattresses were too springy and Jacob Groz, playing Douglas Hadow, bounced clean out of the cloud into the front row of the stalls. At another, the carbon dioxide content of the cloud was too high and the audience was in grave danger of suffocation.

O FEIJÃO DOURADO DA MORTE

(The Golden Bean of Death)

Brazil, 1869

It caused a revolution, the fall of an empire and the banning of all musical theatre throughout Brazil: such is the unique distinction of Antônio Carlos Gomes' operetta *O feijão dourado da morte*. How could a gay and insouciant piece with catchy tunes and choruses lively enough to rival Offenbach's *La Vie Parisienne* have such momentous consequences? What was its fatal charm?

In 1869 the economy of the Brazilian Empire was booming – a bonanza based on the coffee bean. The foremost coffee millionaire Alfredo Mananas built the opera house of Santos[1] and commissioned Gomes, the leading Brazilian composer, whose Italianate operas with national themes were very successful in Europe, to write a work for the opening night. The libretto by Fernandes Dos Reis is the story of rival coffee planters, their struggles to grow the perfect bean, put down slave rebellions, defeat the Paraguayan dictator and win the heart of the sultry Empress of Eldorado.

In the final scene the villain, Delgado, plans to kill Carlos, the hero, with an exploding coffee pot. At rehearsal the bang was judged a feeble anti-climax, and the director decided to boost the effect with an extra bag of gunpowder. Unbeknown to him, the male members of the chorus then added to the pot two or three cartridges from their pistols, but unfortunately neglected to tell each other that they had done so.

The performance, with the Emperor Pedro II in the Imperial Box, seemed set to be a great success, until it came to the final scene, when Delgado dropped his cigar into the coffee pot packed with explosives. The violent detonation killed most of the cast and brought the exuberant plaster ceiling of the auditorium down on the audience of coffee magnates and their mistresses. Somehow Pedro II escaped unscathed, which was taken as evidence that he was behind a plot to kill his political rival, Mananas. The consequent surge of popular anger brought revolution and an end to the Empire of Brazil. The new republican government at once passed a law banning all musical theatre.[2] The opera has never been performed since, and the manuscript was lost when the National Museum of Brazil was destroyed by fire in 2018.

---

1 At that time 90% of the world's coffee passed through the port of Santos.
2 Only the annual Gilbert and Sullivan performance at the British Embassy was exempt.

O FEIJÃO DOURADO DA MORTE

The Brazilian-German Heldentenor Gunther Jose Hinstrich played Carlos. The role of the evil Delgado was sung by the Patagonian-Welsh bass-baritone Francisco Geraint ap Williams. The Empress of Eldorado was acted by the society beauty and serial mistress Victoria Maria Braganza, but the part was sung from behind a moving, many-fronded palm by Ermentrude Botesdale, a thrillingly voiced but very plain English soprano.

* **************

(The Lucky Card)

Hungary, 1885

NO OPERA HAS SUCH an inappropriate title than this. It is the world's most unfortunate and ill-starred opera, its every performance ending in disaster and death. Such is its dread reputation that it is regarded as tempting fate even to mention its name; as the reader will have noticed, alone of all the works in this book this opera is not given its title in the native language. *The Lucky Card* is an approximate translation of the Hungarian, and to say even the English title aloud is regarded by many as too dangerous.[1]

The actual content of the opera is unremarkable: the jolly tale of Janos Kard,[2] a bumptious hussar, who, by the possession of a charmed ace of spades, wins a fortune, survives many duels, gains glory on the battlefield and marries a princess. The music, by Ferenc Erkel,[3] in a welcome departure from his usual ponderously grand style, is sprightly and romantic, and the libretto, by Béni Egressy is witty and even satirical at times.

The first performance was given at the National Opera House in Budapest. Halfway through the second act the tenor, Tibor Lazlo, while singing a complicated but not particularly athletic aria, had a heart attack on a high C and dropped dead centre stage. The next night the performance had reached the final act when the baritone, playing a dastardly major of dragoons, raised his fists to curse heaven and a stagehand promptly fell from the fly tower and crushed him. It was not third time lucky, either, when an inebriated industrialist tumbled from his box into the stalls.

At a later performance in Prague one of the duelling pistols was inadvertently loaded; at La Scala, an overweight princess fell through the stage; and in Dresden a member of the chorus was stabbed. In Berlin the descending iron safety curtain cut off the foot of the famed soprano Magda Heinkel. The last ever performance was given at Vienna, and ended when the tenor was thrown by his mechanical horse into the orchestra pit and impaled on a music stand. This was immediately followed by the announcement that Archduke Rudolf had shot himself and his mistress at Mayerling.

From 1889 for over a century the opera was shunned until, in 1991, the Opera Society in Jetmore, Kansas, daringly attempted a sing-through to the piano score. This was abruptly ended during the second act by a particularly violent and destructive tornado.

---

1 If the reader is worried that they have pronounced the name out loud they should touch the middle button of their shirt or blouse and tug their left and right earlobes in succession.
2 'Kard' means 'sword' in Hungarian. The Hungarian for 'card' is 'kártya'.
3 As well as being the founding father of Hungarian Grand Opera and the writer of the national anthem, Erkel was an international chess and bridge player.

✳ ✳✳✳✳✳✳✳✳✳✳✳✳

In this scene Janos fights a duel with the charwoman of the colonel of the infamous Black Hussars. Janos is given the right to draw a card to determine his opponent and weapon and his lucky ace ensures he does not meet any of the regiment's crack shots or champion swordsmen. Even though no lethal weapons were used in this scene it could not escape the curse of the opera when, at Meiningen, a bucket was kicked into the orchestra, severely injuring the conductor Hans Richter.

LA MARMITE VIDE

(The Empty Casserole)

France, 1891

What could better represent the French love of both *le grandeur* and *la gloire* than a posthumous collaboration of Balzac and Berlioz[1] in an opera so gigantic in scale and scope as to make the grandest of grand opera seem like a parlour performance. In 1891 the industrialist Alphonse Le Creuset, eager to match his commercial success with artistic acclaim, commissioned an opera based on Balzac's Napoleonic epic, *La Marmite Vide*, with music adapted from Berlioz's incomplete and unperformed works: *The Last Day of the World*, *The Death of Hercules* and *Robin Hood*. The Paris Opera was far too small for the ambitious production, and it was staged in the enormous Palais des Machines[2] that stood beside the Eiffel Tower. Le Creuset was convinced that the success of the opera would be as huge as the venue, and a splendid advertisement for his cooking pots, which were displayed prominently in every scene.

Balzac's novel was adapted by the playwright Henri Buguet. It is the story of the Battle of Waterloo, told through the amorous antics of a band of cantinières hawking their pots of stew, which revive the courage and martial ardour of the French army. All ends in a grand cavalry charge; the Dutch and Prussians run away while the British surrender. Wellington is exiled to a barren rock off Brittany, and his horse ends up in the cooking pot to provide a celebratory meal for Napoleon and his Imperial Guard – another culinary masterpiece to complement Chicken Marengo.[3] This improbable version of history is explained as the opium-fuelled fantasy of a starving poet.

There was a *grande armée* of musicians: an orchestra of 521 – including 120 violins, six giant octobasses, forty double-basses, thirty harps, sixteen saxophones and a steam-powered organ – and a cast of forty principals, backed by a chorus of 1,200, including a choir of orphans.[4] What was predicted to be the greatest operatic triumph of the century was instead a debacle to rival the Franco-Prussian War. Buguet selected the most boring bits of Balzac's novel and Berlioz's music was all bombast without any brio. The orchestra deafened the audience, the glass roof shattered and the 100 horses on stage were so frightened they voided their bowels. During the interval news spread that General Boulanger had been shot and a coup d'état was under way[5]. The cast and audience fled, and the performance was never restarted.

---

1 Honoré de Balzac died in 1850; Hector Berlioz died in 1869.
2 The Palais des Machines was built for the Universal Exhibition of 1889. At the time it was the largest enclosed space in the world, spanning over 360 feet (110 m) wide, 1378 feet (420 m) long and 150 feet (45 m) high.
3 A dish named after Napoleon's victory at Marengo in 1800. Napoleon's horse was also called Marengo.
4 Berlioz had a theory that a person's state in life – father, widow, bankrupt, orphan – gave a particular resonance and timbre to the singing voice.
5 Boulanger was indeed shot, but by his own hand, and upon the grave of his late mistress in Brussels.

LA MARMITE VIDE

The cantinières Berthe and Marianne nourish the hard-pressed troops of Marshal Ney with casseroles, and attempt to cheer them up with the rousing aria 'Your Sweethearts Will Polish the Glass of Your Crêpe-Garlanded Portrait With Tears of Pride'.

TEKI NI CHIKADZUKU

(Closer to the Enemy)

Japan, 1895

IT IS SAID THAT when the Japanese, newly opened to the world after four centuries of isolation, built their first copy of a European ship, the replica was so indiscriminatingly exact that it included dents in the hull, patches on the boiler and the scratches made by the ship's cat on the wheelhouse door. This scrupulous fidelity to the original pattern was also applied to the first Japanese attempts at European opera.

A group of officers from the Royal Navy had gone to Japan in the 1870s to teach the techniques and tactics of modern maritime warfare. When they left, the infant Japanese Imperial Navy was thoroughly versed in British naval tradition and enthralled by the operettas of Gilbert and Sullivan.

Japanese sailors were apt pupils, and their new navy destroyed the Chinese fleet at the Battle of the Yalu River in 1894. To celebrate, the Japanese commander-in-chief, Admiral Itō, commissioned an opera closely based on *HMS Pinafore*, which he knew and loved from performances given by his British teachers. *Closer to the Enemy* – originally titled *The Armoured Chrysanthemum* – was the first modern opera to be performed in Japan. The emperor's master of music, Isawa Shūji, diligently copied the incomplete score left by the Royal Navy, inadvertently including all the errors as well as inserting 'Auld Lang Syne',[1] 'For He's a Jolly Good Fellow' and several indelicate sea shanties.

Admiral Itō insisted on minor changes to the text. The pirates became Koreans, the sisters and aunts geishas, and 'I am the Model of a Modern Major-General' was omitted as a potential insult to the army. A middle act was added where the sailor Deadeye Dick, mistranslated as One-Eyed Hitachi, failed to see the signal ordering retreat and ordered his ship to ram the Chinese flagship. On the first night this was so popular that twelve encores were demanded and the Chinese ship was reduced to splinters.

The opera was a rollicking success with the Japanese navy and general public. It soon became a tradition that 'We Sail the Ocean Blue' was sung each morning on every warship after the raising of the Imperial flag. The popularity of the piece was dented when Admiral Tōgō's flagship, *Mikasa*, unexpectedly blew up during a performance on the 10th of September 1905.[2] The opera was thought to be unlucky until the 1920s, when it was actively discouraged and more nationalistic pieces were favoured. But 'With Catlike Tread' could still be heard in Japanese submarines until the end of the Second World War.

---

1 Extraordinarily popular in Japan, it is now the custom to play *Auld Lang Syne* as department stores close for the day.
2 The *Mikasa* was the flagship of the fleet that annihilated the Russian fleet at the Battle of Tsushima the previous year. The explosion was at first blamed either on sailors resentful of the terms of the peace treaty that ended the Russo-Japanese War or disgruntled actors from the traditional Noh theatre. The true cause was later found to be defective ammunition.

In the final thrilling scene One-Eyed Hitachi urges his shipmates to break off their chorus of heroic resolve to attack the enemy. The chorus member with the rope was a master of a rope-tying art, which, while it did not add anything to the drama, gave him something to do while on stage: a perpetual problem for members of the chorus that directors solve in many ingenious ways.

The sets, designed and painted by the noted artist Kobayashi Kiyochika, were mounted on an ingenious panoramic apparatus called the Mareorama. It was designed in France but built by Mitsubishi. To simulate the roll and pitch of a ship the whole auditorium was mounted on Cardanic rings similar to those used for mounting ships' compasses. This involved the use of floats in water, hydraulic piston engines and pumps driven by electric motors. Electricity and water are a dangerous combination and, after several unfortunate incidents, the apparatus was scrapped.

AABHAAREE HO

(Count Your Blessings)

India, 1904

Many operas have been set in India, but there is only one on record that was written by an Indian. *Aabhaaree Ho*, by the telegraph clerk and mathematical genius Pathani Mukherjee, is the unique, but unsuccessful, example. Mukherjee moved to London in 1901 to aid Bertrand Russell on his *Principia Mathematica*. He had gained a taste for western music from military bands and the East Bengal Railway Choir,[1] and, after discovering the delights of the London music halls, decided to write an opera. He wrote it in two weeks while continuing to work on laborious calculations for Russell.

The plot is reminiscent of a story from *The Boy's Own Paper*, of which Mukherjee had grown up reading tattered back copies. A peasant boy of noble character and formidable intellect defeats the machinations of thuggees to qualify as a doctor and bring the benefits of vaccination and the bicycle to the jungles of East Bengal. The music was extraordinarily complex, both harmonically and rhythmically, constructed from the mathematical relationship of prime numbers to conic sections.

The first performance, given before an advanced and enlightened London audience, failed to please on every front. Mukherjee's open enthusiasm for the benefits of the British Raj – citing railways, printing presses, hypodermic syringes and tin openers – irritated the anti-imperialists, while his blatant materialism appalled the mystics and devotees of Indian spiritualism. The orchestration was too experimental even for those eager to embrace the latest fads, and the lyrics, sung in Sanskrit, English and Hindi, were incomprehensible on every level. After Lytton Strachey was bitten by a snake and D.H. Lawrence refused a second complimentary glass of Desi daru, Bloomsbury turned its back on Mukherjee and his opera. It was never heard again.

---

1 The choir was founded soon after the opening of the railway in 1857.

A crucial scene in the opera where Doctor Tandori confounds an obscurantist fakir with exponential equations was ruined when a violent altercation began between Lady Ottoline Morell, Virginia Stephen[1] and those in the second row who complained of their view being obstructed by the women's extravagant hats.

---

[1] Better known as Virginia Woolf after her marriage to Leonard Woolf in 1912.

KRAKEN

(The Kraken)

Denmark, 1905

To produce any opera outdoors is to tempt fate, but to stage one on the rusty hulk of a capsised battleship in the middle of a wave-swept harbour is to recklessly court disaster. These were the circumstances that made the 1904 performance of *Kraken* a humiliation to match the Danish defeat by the Prussians in 1864. To celebrate the marriage of Princess Ingeborg to the Duke of Västergötland and Denmark's presidency of the Scandinavian Fishery League, the Copenhagen Royal Opera House commissioned an opera – not a mere light-hearted courtly diversion, but an ambitious and enormous epic. The composer Harald Guldorgsund collaborated with the folklorist Herluf Trolle, to produce a seven-hour epic whose grandiose score out-Wagnered Wagner. *Kraken* was based on the legendary conflict between Bishop Sygge of Borglum, who celebrated Mass on the back of the gigantic sea monster and wished to baptise it, and King Olaf Snaggletooth, who wanted to train it to destroy his enemies.

A romantic interest, in the shapely form of a mermaid princess, was introduced to lighten what was, even by Scandinavian standards, a sombre and dismally serious piece.

The expressionist stage designer Hans Christian Dannebrog used the upturned bottom of the ironclad *Skjold*[1] lying in the middle of Copenhagen harbour as a vast barnacle-encrusted stage. The singers stood, with some difficulty, on the rusty hulk, the orchestra was placed on a nearby raft, while gigantic horns, fashioned from the ship's boiler tubes, were played inside the hull. Also inside was the Russian basso profundo Alexandr Petropavlosk as the voice of the Kraken.

The night of the performance was cold, with a sharp wind and corrugated waves. Sandi Tostvig, the 'Danish Nightingale', singing the part of the mermaid, was seasick; the famed tenor Olfert Fischer lost his voice, never to regain it; and Petropavlosk suffered acute claustrophobia. His amplified bellows drowned out the rest of the singers – some critics said this was the best part of the opera – and he had to be rescued with flame-cutting torches. The performance was abandoned after two hours when the orchestra raft broke loose and drifted into the Skagerrak and Princess Ingeborg was carried away with what later developed into pneumonia.

The dejected and disgraced Guldorgsund fled to America, where he had an unexpected second career as a composer for early silent films and an orchestrator for Jerome Kern.

---

1 A 3,000-ton coast-defence battleship, *Skjold*, had capsised due to a serious miscalculation of the weight of her superstructure.

The bishop, the captain of the king's guard and the mermaid princess sing a lullaby to the Kraken. The soporific qualities of the lullaby were so successful that not only did many of the audience fall asleep, but so did several members of the chorus. One, unfortunately wearing a heavy suit of chain mail, fell off the stage into the harbour.

MALLEUS HAERETICORUM

(The Hammer of the Heretics)

The Vatican, 1912

Within the walls of the Vatican are not just churches, museums and convents but a radio station, a railway station, a police station and Italy's smallest and most opulent opera house: Santa Cecilia. The architect was that universal baroque genius, Gian Lorenzo Bernini, who carved much of the sculptural decoration, painted the ceiling, designed the costumes and wrote the libretti of many of the operas performed there. It has only seventy (extremely comfortable) seats, matching the number of cardinals when it was built in 1665. However, it has been disused since the disastrous performance on the 14th of April 1912[1] of *Malleus haereticorum*, the longest, least tuneful and certainly the dullest opera ever performed in Italy. This ponderous work of pious tedium was commissioned by Pope Pius X who, as well as persecuting liberal theologians, commanded all church music should be Gregorian chant and sung only by all-male choirs.

Instead of closing the opera house the Pope insisted on a work of suitable gravity. The subject he chose was the bitter struggle between orthodox Catholics and Arian heretics in the fourth century AD. Unfortunately the Latin libretto was of formidable erudition and minimal dramatic interest, concentrating on the subtlest nuances of theology. A twenty-minute recitative on the exact meaning of the word 'from' was not the best way to hold an audience's attention. The music, scored only for pipe organ and liturgical bells, was by Don Perosi, Director of the Sistine Chapel Choir. Apart from the lack of any melodies, another obstacle to popular success was the ban on women. The only female characters, the Virgin Mary, the Empress Theodora and St Emphysimia of Naxos, were played by elderly castrati.

The performance ended when a halberd, dropped by a dozing Swiss Guard, struck Cardinal Cavalcanti on the head.[2] The commotion awoke the rest of the cardinals, except one, who had slipped into such a profound coma that nothing, not even the application of Galvani's electrical apparatus, could revive him. *Malleus haereticorum* was given the last rites that night as well. The Pope ordered the manuscript to be placed in the secret archives of the Vatican where, presumably, it still remains, along with the poison recipes of Lucrezia Borgia, the Third Secret of Fátima and Mary Magdalene's marriage licence.

---

1 On the same night the *Titanic* struck an iceberg.
2 Joaquim Arcoverde de Albuquerque Cavalcanti was the first South American cardinal. He was unhurt, as his cardinal's hat was reinforced with steel. The cardinal had a morbid fear of assassination by anti-clerical anarchists and Freemasons, and he always wore chain mail under his vestments.

Here Athanasius, played by Beniamino Gigli, seeks the support of the Empress Theodora in his struggle against the arch-heretic Basil of Ancyrato. The empress was sung by the castrato Alessandro Moreschi and the young angel was played by a boy from the Sistine Chapel Choir, Annibale Bergonzoli. When his voice broke, Annibale joined the army and served with distinction in both World Wars and the Spanish Civil War. By then he had a fine baritone and bristling beard which gave him his nickname, Barba Elettrica ('Electric Beard'). His stirring performances of patriotic arias failed to stiffen the resolve of his troops, and he was forced to surrender to the Eighth Army in 1941.[1] The scenery was designed and painted by a young Giorgio de Chirico, whose austere and mysterious metaphysical paintings had impressed the Pope when he saw them in a Turin gallery.

---

[1] General Bergonzoli's luxuriously appointed caravan was appropriated by General Montgomery, who appreciated its comforts but not the giant gramophone and collection of opera records. These were taken by General Alexander, who did. The caravan survives in the Imperial War Museum collection at Duxford.

OBŘÍ KAPR

(The Enormous Carp)

Bohemia, 1913

There is only one opera where the principal character is a fish – probably one too many. *Obří kapr* was commissioned in 1913 by Octavia, the wife of František Škoda, head of that great engineering and armaments firm. An opera lover and Czech nationalist, Octavia wanted an opera in Czech about angling, as her husband was a keen fisherman. However, she was badly advised to give the commission to the chromatic symbolist Balthazar Zatopek, with a libretto by the journalist and practical joker Jaroslav Hašek.[1]

They produced a surreal work in which an insurance clerk, Miroslav, falls in love with a nun, Jelona, and so is condemned to live at the bottom of a fishpond in the form of a carp. But, if he is caught by one who is pure, who has never travelled by tram or eaten meat, he will regain human form. Although Miroslav is often hooked, none of the anglers fulfil the conditions, and he continues to lurk in the pond, growing ever larger.

At last Miroslav is caught by Jelona, who, bored with being a nun, has become a trapeze artist. She fulfils all the conditions, and Miroslav is about to be restored to mortal form and its associated anticipated conjugal bliss, but everything is lost, as she eats a sausage that she mistakes for a gherkin. Miroslav, still an enormous carp, is carried away by boys from the reformatory to be cooked and eaten in an interminable scene that sets every recipe for carp to music's longest contrapuntal fugue.

The opera's first night at the National Theatre, Prague, was a disaster: Kafka, who should have reviewed it, was laid low by nosebleeds; Mahler, who was to conduct, was literally derailed on the way from Vienna; the replacement conductor, the famously myopic Otakar Rozladeny, stood on his spectacles; the carp pool leaked, fused the lights and flooded the orchestra pit. Madame Škoda's only comment was: 'But I thought it would be like *The Bartered Bride*.' A fragment of the music still occasionally heard is a dissonant polka that was used as the theme for the 1950s Czech puppet show *Pratelsky Pavouk*.[2]

---

1 Hašek was the editor of the magazine *Animal World*, where he spent most of his time trying unsuccessfully to teach flies how to perform tricks.
2 'The Friendly Spider'.

The sets and costumes were designed by Josef Lada, the Czech artist most famous for his illustrations to Hašek's comic novel *The Good Soldier Švejk*. The giant carp was bought by the famous restaurant U Malířů, where it decorated the main dining room until its destruction by the Gestapo during the Second World War. Reinhard Heydrich, the Reich Protector of Bohemia, had become convinced that it was a subversive representation of Himmler.

GIGANTSKAYA KURSKAYA GUSENITSA

(The Giant Caterpillar of Kursk)

The Union of Soviet Socialist Republics, 1931

I T WAS VERY HARD BEING a composer in Russia after the revolution – although probably not as hard as being a peasant in Siberia. Following the ever-shifting party line was as difficult as playing Ligetti's *Études*. The initial enthusiasm of the Bolsheviks for progressive and avant-garde music was soon replaced by a demand for the simple and serviceable melodies of socialist realism. If a composer wanted to continue making music he – and it was overwhelmingly he, despite the Bolsheviks' proclamations of sexual equality – had to join the Russian Association of Proletarian Musicians. This was difficult for the aristocratic Alexander Vorontsov, whose grandmother had been a pupil and mistress of Liszt and who was the only conductor to have a baton made by Fabergé.[1] He solved the problem by swapping identities with the blacksmith from the former family estate, and became Yuri Kuznetsov. He won great popular success with songs celebrating the abundant harvest and the overproduction of dynamos.

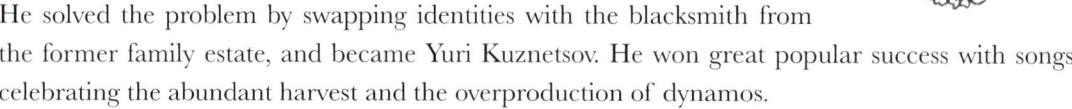

In 1931 Kuznetsov wrote his only opera, which was to be staged at the Bolshoi and then to tour factories throughout the USSR. The libretto, of commendably rugged proletarian aspect, was by Feodor Gladkov.[2] *The Giant Caterpillar of Kursk* was not some whimsical folktale, but a stark and heroic epic of noble proletarian mechanics struggling to build an agricultural tractor with caterpillar tracks powered by electricity. They were continually thwarted, and their prototype was sabotaged by reactionary bourgeois counter-revolutionaries building a rival petrol-engined, wheeled tractor.

The music was melodic, solid and conventional, although the counter-revolutionaries were allowed more complex and progressive themes to illustrate their deviance and decadence.

Popular success was certain, but unfortunately the theme offended Stalin, who abruptly decided that only diesel tractors were truly proletarian. Stalin's glowering looks of disapproval from his box in the Bolshoi so unnerved the cast that wrong notes and missed cues marred the performance until it eventually stuttered to an end. There was no applause. Soon afterwards, everyone connected with the production was accused of technical deviationism, purged and sent to the Gulag where, ironically, most ended up in a tractor factory.

---

1 Lost for many years, the baton was rediscovered on a 2006 edition of the *Antiques Roadshow* broadcast from Symphony Hall, Birmingham.
2 A prolific writer, the works of Feodor Vasilyevich Gladkov include *Cement* (1925), *Energy* (1932–38) and *The Old Secret Prison* (1926).

GIGANTSKAYA KURSKAYA GUSENITSA

Here Pytor, the tractor factory's comrade designer, sets the controls of the mighty agricultural machine aided by Natasha – a comely cam-shaft grinder who provides a quota of ideologically correct glamour – watched by a resentful and suspicious committee of deviationists, intent on sabotage. Despite the obvious attraction of the two principals, all overt romance was sublimated to the over-achievement of production targets.

THE WALSINGHAM WAY

(The Walsingham Way)

England, 1932

There have been many operas about journeys, of which Rossini's *Il viaggio a Reims* is certainly the most melodic. However, there has only been one opera in which the whole cast and audience processed through the countryside. This dubious distinction falls to *The Walsingham Way*, which had one disastrous outing in rural Norfolk.

In August 1932, to celebrate the opening of the Anglo-Catholic Shrine of Our Lady of Walsingham, Dame Sybil Thorndike[1] proposed an operatic pageant, which would tell the story of the Shrine from its medieval origins. The procession would start at the Slipper Chapel, one mile from Walsingham, and would then wend its tuneful way through the lanes to the Abbey in the town.

T.S. Eliot[2] penned the libretto, and Dame Ethel Smyth wrote the music. Eliot's verse, written in haste, was barely adequate, and it was generally admitted that the parts of the score that did not sound like *The March of the Women* were all too similar to *Greensleeves*. The star, Our Lady of Walsingham herself, was to be carried on a litter and to sing duets with various pilgrims along the way. The part was first offered to Lady Diana Cooper, who had played the Virgin Mary in Max Rheinhardt's blockbuster *The Miracle*. She turned down the opportunity as she could not sing, and the part was offered to Dame Clara Butt, whose enormous voice was thought suitable for the al fresco setting.

The first and only performance was eagerly anticipated – only to end in disaster. As both cast and audience were required to process barefoot along the Holy Mile, many quickly fell out lame. The Sea Scouts carrying Dame Clara, whose already substantial bulk was increased by a heavy embroidered cope and golden crown, wilted under their burden, and she was transferred to a small hay cart. It then began to rain heavily and, as the depleted and bedraggled ensemble approached Walsingham, they were buzzed by practising RAF bombers. The donkeys bearing two of the three Magi bolted, which made the presence of the final Wise Man somewhat pointless.

Finally, arriving late at the Abbey gate, the opera clashed with an Anglo-Catholic pilgrimage trying to get in and a pious band of Roman Catholics trying to get out. After a long and trying day, Christian charity was in short supply. Tempers frayed and fists flew. The fracas was joined by some Russian Orthodox monks and a gang of Kensitites – a militant and aggressive band of Anglo Anti-Catholics. The battle raged about the gate and up the High Street to the Market Place, and was only quelled after extra police were brought in from Fakenham and Wells. 'The only miracle that day,' Dame Sybil remarked, 'was that nobody was killed.'

---

1 Dame Sybil was a noted Anglo-Catholic, although she combined this with, for the time, very left-wing politics. She would have liked the leading role for herself, but it took a miracle for her to sing in tune.

2 Many writers at the time – Graham Greene, Evelyn Waugh, G.K. Chesterton – became Roman Catholics, but Eliot, ever the contrarian, became an Anglo-Catholic.

John Tolkien, son of J.R.R. Tolkien, was a member the Roman Catholic pilgrimage and an enthusiastic participant in the conflict. He received a cut lip and a black eye, but always asserted that he gave as good as he got. Tolkien scholars believe that his account of the fracas inspired his father to write the passage describing the epic battle of the five armies in his 1937 masterpiece, *The Hobbit*. This is the only existing photograph of the holy fracas, taken by the village photographer, Kenneth Faircloth, whose shop was directly opposite the Abbey gate. Over a long career he took thousands of photographs of pious pilgrims, but always maintained this was his favourite. Needless to say, there is not a copy in the Archives of the Shrine of Our Lady of Walsingham, and existing prints are very, very rare.

DER FLIEGENDE HAMBURGER

(The Flying Hamburger)

Germany, 1933

This opera is not, as you might think, about fast food, but a fast train. With music as elegant and modern as one of Erich Mendelsohn's department stores, *Der Fliegende Hamburger*, the best of the short-lived *Zeitoper* genre, is a perfect evocation of the bittersweet world of Weimar Germany, with schmaltz and cynicism blended to perfection. Set on the legendary *Flying Hamburger* diesel train[1], then the fastest in the world, this is a witty and tuneful tale of robbery, sabotage and blighted passion, involving a cabaret artiste, two spies, a boy detective and a theoretical physicist.

The music was by the 'Wunderkind of Wuttenberg' Max Peenemunde.[2] He had studied with Webern and was a close associate of Hindemith, but his love of the nightclubs of Berlin saved him from the arid temptations of Modernism. Buried in the score is the only successful musical example of Heisenberg's Uncertainty Principle, but the rest of the music is, in the words of the *Berliner Tageblatt*, 'like Strauss in suspenders.'

The witty libretto was by the dramatist and stunt pilot Erich von Stalheim, with whom Peenemunde often went wing-walking.[3] There were sly but safe allusions to contemporary politics, cocaine and cross-dressing, which allowed the audience to feel comfortably enlightened. The plot hinges on the efforts of the physicist Dr Caligari – a dangerous communist – to sabotage the railway timetable by manipulating relativity. He is thwarted by a young Adolf, aided by the exotic dancer, Eva. Two bungling spies – one French and the other British – provide the comedy.

Unlike that other railway-based opera, *Long, Long Train o' Misery*, *Der Fliegende Hamburger* was a resounding success: far too successful, in fact, and unfortunate in its fans: Goebbels loved it; it was Göring's favourite opera (he was a keen railway modeller); and Hitler, who also liked trains, saw it three times and had a recording of it with him in the final bunker. It was banned during the post-war denazification programme and, with the dubious distinction of being the only opera ever to have been made illegal, has never been heard again.

---

1 *The Flying Hamburger* was a streamlined, lightweight two-carriage express train. It carried one hundred passengers between Berlin and Hamburg. With diesel-electric propulsion it achieved the record average speed of seventy-seven miles an hour.

2 Peenemunde joined the Luftwaffe in 1935 as Chief Musical Advisor, and it was he who tuned the sirens of the Stuka dive-bomber to the terrifying banshee wail that formed the soundtrack to the Blitzkrieg. When war broke out he could not resist flying, and was shot down over Kent in September 1940. By an odd coincidence he was captured by the composer Constant Lambert, who was in the Home Guard at Bexley.

3 Peenemunde was not content with merely walking on the wing of a flying aeroplane. He regularly played tennis, often tap danced with the chorus of the Kit Kat Klub and premiered his second piano trio over Nuremberg on the wing of a Heinkel He 72.

The cast pose for an inaugural photograph. Dr Caligari's aurora of wild hair was sustained by a miniature Van der Graaff generator concealed in his briefcase. Eva is emerging from her Infinite Cabin Trunk. Young Adolf's sweater was so popular that its knitting pattern outsold all others until the outbreak of war in 1939. The builders of the *Flying Hamburger*, Waggon-und-Maschinenbau AG, contributed a full-sized front section with air horns specially tuned by the composer himself. A limited-edition trainset by Märklin, with miniature figures of all the characters, was popular at the time, and commands a very high price at auction today.

THE ROUGH AND THE FAIR

(The Rough and the Fair)

England, 1934

'WE HAVE MODERN ART, modern architecture, modern music, modern literature and modern morals – but why no modern opera?' queried George Bernard Shaw in a 1934 radio broadcast. On hearing this Lilian Baylis of the Old Vic and Sadlers Wells theatres asked Benjamin Britten to write an opera set on a Travelling Post Office train. He declined when he discovered she had rejected W.H. Auden's libretto for one by P.G. Wodehouse, which changed the scene to a golf course. The music was then composed by Lord Haversack.[1]

The *Rough and the Fair* is an opera in eighteen scenes. Set on a golf course 'up North', it is a tale of class conflict and thwarted passion. The hero, Bert Scrope, leads the artisan members of the club in their revolutionary struggle to play in the afternoon. Bert is the lover of Angela Mowbray Hunt, the ladies' captain and fiancée of Archibald Stokes Mortar, the owner of an armaments factory.

The music is romantic classical whimsy, wrapped in swathes of modish atonalism. The scenes are set on successive holes, each with a musical theme made up of the number of chords to match that of the hole. It was not exactly tuneful. Wodehouse said Haversack's treatment of a melody was 'like a man who bought himself a kitten to practise vivisection on.'

The production was beset with squabbles between Wodehouse and the director, Tyrone Guthrie, over the accuracy of golf shots, while Lilian Baylis rowed with Haversack over his lunch bills and the persistent, giggling presence of Cecil Beaton at rehearsals.

The run was doomed from the outset, with facetious first-night reviews coming in: 'Just up to scratch' and 'Below par but will make the cut.'

Disaster struck on the fourth night, when the Prince of Wales and Mrs Simpson attended. Joan Cross, singing Angela, sliced her stroke and shot the ball into the royal box, where it knocked Mrs Simpson unconscious. As she slumped over the balcony, her necklace broke and cascaded into the stalls. 'Pearls before swine!' bellowed Sir Thomas Beecham gleefully. The Prince of Wales jumped down to the stage and tried to brain Joan Cross with a niblick, but was whacked into the orchestra pit with a driving iron wielded by Peter Pears.

Although the debacle was social rather than musical, the opera soon closed and has never been performed since.

---

1 Lord Haversack was England's second titled composer. The other was Lord Berners. There was great rivalry between them in matters both musical and motoring. Haversack trumped Berners – who had a Rolls Royce fitted with a small harpsichord – by equipping his gigantic Bugatti Royale with a half-sized Wurlitzer cinema organ.

One fortunate consequence of Peter Pears' involvement in the ill-fated opera was that he fell in love with golf, eventually becoming a scratch player. It was his secret passion for the game that made him persuade Benjamin Britten to move from Crag House on the sea front at Aldeburgh to the Red House, which adjoined the golf links.

LONG, LONG TRAIN O' MISERY

(Long, Long Train o' Misery)

The United States of America, 1936

AMONGST THE MANY MILLIONS made destitute in the Great Depression were thousands of musicians. One of the many agencies set up by President Roosevelt in his New Deal was the Federal Music Project,[1] designed to give employment to performers and composers. The Project's most ambitious undertaking was the opera *Long, Long Train o' Misery*, a tale of 'hobos bumming their way west' on a freight train. Ruth Seeger wrote the music and the libretto was by the Federal Writing Project.[2]

The hobos occupied a train of boxcars, from which they sang their songs of pain and woe. The number of scenes varied, according to the musicians available, the size of the theatre and the audience's stamina. The shortest performance had six scenes, the longest sixty-eight. Some cars were crammed with characters – usually the unemployed choruses of bankrupt theatres – while others housed solitary tramps who, despite their privations, sang at length about the wickedness of Wall Street. A young Pete Seeger played a blacklisted docker given to interminable banjo solos.

The setting was simple: a backdrop showing a wind-swept, desolate prairie with a length of railway track across the stage. During the overture the locomotive appeared, followed by the boxcars and their human freight, to end with a caboose filled with a chorus of carousing train crew. George Balanchine choreographed the ballet of brutal guards who patrolled the roofs with fine percussive effects. Romance was provided by a tender scene between a starving fruit picker, played by Woody Guthrie, and a consumptive librarian.

Despite the praise of East Coast critics, the opera failed to woo the public, who preferred the extravagant musicals of Busby Berkeley. To the Republican opponents of Roosevelt this proved the superiority of the free market as opposed to government-directed projects, but the real cause of the opera's failure was artistic, not political. It was very worthy, but extremely dull. Each performance was like being stuck at a level crossing while a very long train trundled slowly past; the music was monotonous and the quality of much of the acting and singing justly demonstrated why the artists were unemployed. But ultimately it was felt that there was just too much misery, and people had quite enough of that at home. After one nationwide tour the opera was soon forgotten, except for several numbers that Pete Seeger adapted for his folk group The Weavers, and in 1968 Phil Spector produced 'The Dust Bowl of My Soul' for The Righteous Brothers.

---

1 The Federal Music Project was formed in 1935 to support musicians during the Depression. It was wound up in 1940. Some claim this was a direct result of the *Long, Long Train o' Misery*.
2 As they all demanded a credit, the opera is the only one where the list of librettists is longer than the libretto itself.

LONG, LONG TRAIN O' MISERY

Here the docker, Jack Ironfist, played by Pete Seeger, is accompanied by two hobos in 'That Slow ol' Iron Horse is A-draggin' Me West'. Usually Seeger sang and played alone. The boxcars were real ones, salvaged from the bankrupt Abilene, Salina and Great Bend Railroad.

OPERA ANTARCTICA

(Antarctic Opera)

Antarctica, 1950

Vaughan Williams wrote the music for the 1948 film *Scott of the Antarctic*. It was so much admired that he adapted the score to form his seventh symphony: *Sinfonia antarctica*. Before this was finished he was approached by Daniel Webster, Chief Executive of the Royal Opera House, who suggested an opera on the same bleak subject. A heroic but doomed struggle in freezing conditions was judged to be just the thing that post-war austerity Britain needed.

After an unsuccessful initial collaboration with A.A. Milne, Vaughan Williams worked with a libretto written by Montagu Slater. Slater had written the libretto of Britten's *Peter Grimes*, but had fallen out with the composer. Knowing that Vaughan Williams was Britten's least favourite composer after Brahms, Slater was only too happy to work with him.

The first performance was scheduled for January 1950, with William MacAlpine as Captain Scott and bass David Ward as Chief Petty Officer Evans. The only female characters were Scott's wife Kathleen – sung by Kathleen Ferrier – and a troupe of dancing girls who appeared in dream sequences.

Rehearsals were under way and going well, apart from an unfortunate tendency of the over-powerful wind machine[1] to blow Captain Oates back onstage after he had made his exit singing his poignant farewell aria, 'I May Be Away Some Time'. Alas, two days before the opening night, the opera house's ancient heating system broke down. Faced with icicles in the dress circle and temperatures backstage nearly as low as those in the Antarctic itself, the performance was reluctantly postponed. Sadly, future scheduling conflicts meant that it was never staged.

There was a recording made later in the year at the Kingsway Hall, Holborn. Unfortunately, this coincided with an unprecedented heatwave. The hall's ventilation system broke down and, as the doors had to be left open, many a moment of stark drama was marred by the cheerful shouts of newspaper boys and bus conductors that the recording engineers never quite managed to suppress.

In 1962 the opera received its only performance, actually in Antarctica. In that year three members of the British Antarctic Survey were opera lovers and enthusiastic amateur musicians. Taking a copy of the recording and a score with them, they resolved to put on a performance in Scott's original hut using his very own piano, which had stood there unplayed for fifty years.[2]

They did their best, but the out-of-tune piano and depressing subject matter cast such a pall of gloom in the freezing hut that after only half an hour the audience demanded an end to the performance. They then tuned in to *Two-Way Family Favourites* to cheer themselves up.

---

1 Designed by Barnes Wallis, the wind machine had been used in testing his less successful invention, the Skipping Bomb. It was so powerful that, if the stage door was open, it blew the baskets from the heads of the Covent Garden Market porters.

2 A patent portable piano made by J.B. Cramer & Co in 1897, now in the Horniman Museum (object no. M7-1991).

This is the only picture of a dress rehearsal at Covent Garden in early January, 1950. It shows Scott and his companions at the South Pole, where they have found Amundsen's tent. Knowing they are beaten, they sing the most depressing quintet in all opera: 'Pipped at the Pole: What Is the Point?' The set was designed by Oliver Messel. After a wartime career disguising pillboxes in Somerset as roadside cafés, cottage ornés and Gothic follies, he began his association with the Royal Opera House in 1946, when he designed the sets and costumes for the Royal Ballet's new production of Tchaikovsky's ballet *The Sleeping Beauty*. This starred Margot Fonteyn, who was greatly offended when asked to be one of the dancing girls in the opera. Questions were asked why the bare white backdrops and drab costumes of *Opera Antarctica* cost exactly the same as the elaborate ballet production and why Messel was paid the same fee. 'Darling, there is white and there is white. It takes real flair to tell the difference,' he told Daniel Webster, whose reply goes unrecorded.

ÄR VI DÄR ÄN?

(Are We There Yet?)

Sweden, 1959

THE CHEERFUL VULGARITY of the Eurovision Song Contest and the bleak austerity of contemporary Swedish opera have little in common, except for one song from Waldemar Oresund's long-forgotten *Är Vi Där Än?*. Oresund – known as the bridge between Sibelius and contemporary Scandinavian music – had a hit opera in 1957, *The Last Temptations*, which was performed throughout the world, and for a sequel in 1959 he collaborated with Ingmar Bergman on *Are We There Yet?*. This bleak allegory was an exhaustive and sombre examination of the tortured Swedish soul, expressed in suitably painful music using minor and diminished intervals in combination with experimental percussion.

The work recounts the journey of a typical Swedish family of four in their Volvo saloon from their Carl Larsson-inspired house amongst the silver birches of Sundborn to a new home buried beneath a grim iron-ore mountain in the far north. On the way they have highly symbolic encounters with various archetypes of Swedish society: child psychiatrists, social workers, ball-bearing manufacturers, nudists and a neurotic elk. These are interspersed with scenes of existential angst and marital friction, concluding in the inevitable chess game played beneath the cruel neon lights of a petrol station.

The climactic scene where the parents are faced with an existentialist dilemma at a fork in the road – on one hand the bright arc lights of the iron mine, on the other the guttering lamps of a woodcutter's hovel – is never resolved, either dramatically or musically.

An uncharacteristically charming and melodic chorus sung by the children gives the title to the whole work. Although the opera did not meet with much success, the titular song, '*Är Vi Där Än?*', was chosen as Sweden's entry to the 1963 Eurovision Song Contest.[1] Later it achieved revived popularity in a Saab advert of the 1970s.

---

1 Even with Monica Zetterland singing, it scored *nul points*, as Norway gave all theirs to Denmark, who won.

Because of the prominence of the chess-playing scene set at a petrol station, the production was originally sponsored by Statoil, the Scandinavian oil company. After seeing the dress rehearsal the company abruptly ended their support, which allowed the designer, Knut Kalmar, to repaint the set in a more appropriate livery.

THE FATAL COMPACT

(The Fatal Compact)

Australia, 1957

Australia in the 1950s was stony ground on which to sow the seeds of modern opera, and *The Fatal Compact*, the first attempt, duly withered and died. It should have been titled *The Fatal Compromise*, for its ambitious attempt to blend indigenous, colonial and European modes of music and drama resulted in a work that confirmed all the robust Australian prejudices against unconventional harmony.

In 1955 Eugene Goossens, the director of the New South Wales State Conservatorium of Music, commissioned a piece to open the new Sydney Opera House. He chose Banjo McKenzie to write the music and Red Greengrass, the poetic voice of the outback, to provide the libretto. The opera was to match the thrilling new forms of the projected opera house and to show the world that Australian culture had struck off its colonial shackles. *The Fatal Compact* was a needlessly complex tale of convicts, gold rushes, tyrannical governors, aboriginal mystics and surfing beatniks, all travelling their idiosyncratic song lines through the wastes of the Nullarbor Desert and the suburbs of Melbourne. The ghost of Ned Kelly materialised at irregular intervals to no apparent purpose. The music was ambitious and omnivorous, with elements of western harmony, Celtic folk tunes, rock and roll, aboriginal modal drones and the percussive possibilities of corrugated iron roofing.

By the time the opera was finished in 1957 the Opera House was still on the drawing board and the first performance was given at Sydney Town Hall. Despite a distinguished cast – Joan Sutherland played a camel-riding doctor and the great Peter Dawson, in his last performance, sang the ghost of Ned Kelly – *The Fatal Compact* failed to please. In the 1950s Australian musical tastes were not sophisticated, and the exotic recipe of coloratura, didgeridoos, electric guitars, Gamelan orchestra and an out-of-tune upright piano proved to be indigestible. The review in *The Sydney Morning Herald* was the one-word headline. STREWTH![1]

---

1 The work, improbably, does have a small band of devoted admirers. They arranged a couple of performances at the historic Teatro Australis (see p. 66) in 2004, and their ultimate goal is to persuade Sydney Opera House to stage a revival, but the management has always ignored them. If you would like to help their campaign please sign their petition to Sydney Opera House at https://renardpress.com/bring-back-the-fatal-compact/.

THE FATAL COMPACT

Sergeant Kennedy embraces the mystic surfer girl Cora Mortmain, who has hitch-hiked through time and desert to be with him. The ghost of Ned Kelly leers through the window. Outside a group of aborigines dance a stately corroboree against the lurid backdrop of a mushroom cloud rising from the site of a nuclear explosion on the Maralinga Atomic Range.

X (O = Z 2 X ; ⊲ 1 0 0 0 . 0) ⊲ X = O / C 2 ⟩

(Reach for the Stars)

International, 1976

MANY A COMPOSER HAS WISHED he could dispense with his librettist, and virtually all librettists think their work is better read than sung, but only one opera has dispensed with both. *Reach for the Stars* is the only opera that has been written completely by computers.

In 1976 the *Voyager 1* was preparing for launch. Previous spacecraft carried plaques identifying their place of origin for the benefit of any aliens that might find them in the future. In this instance, NASA decided on a more ambitious project: a time capsule, consisting of a phonograph record – a twelve-inch gold-plated copper disk containing sounds and images portraying the diversity of life and culture on earth. When this was completed, someone realised that, although the music section contained Bach, Beethoven, Chuck Berry and Peruvian panpipes, there was no opera. Instead of selecting existing extracts, NASA decided to commission a new piece. To avoid the inevitable wrangling over who was best suited to write the work, NASA decided to boldly go for AI.

The ICCAL[1] developed an artificial language for the libretto; the IRCAM[2] adapted their existing programmes to compose the music; and a computer – IBM Bach – was built to write the opera. Nobody was quite sure what the new work would be like until the final printouts. It was certainly novel, although baffling in its complexity. The plot was a weird amalgam of Shakespeare and *Rigoletto*, and the music, with wide, open electronic chords, staccato rhythms and lyrical melodies, resembled, if anything, a combination of Kraftwerk and Puccini.

A distinguished cast – including Grace Bumbry, Marilyn Horne, Samuel Ramey and a very young Renée Fleming – sang, accompanied by an entirely synthetic orchestra, conducted with bemused brio by Leonard Bernstein. The performance was recorded and filmed in a hangar on the ultra-secret Nevada airbase, Area 51.

Loaded on to *Voyager 1*, the opera was blasted into space in 1977, and has been heading for its first audience ever since. It is now fifteen billion miles away, far beyond the heliosphere, and heading for the stars. Will it ever be heard, we have to wonder, as it recedes ever further from earth into the infinite immensities of deep space? Who knows. And coming from the opposite direction an opera might be on its way to us – a work devised by inconceivable intelligences, with rhythms tuned to utterly alien life cycles, in sounds way beyond our aural range, on a subject and in a language that we could not even recognise as such, let alone begin to comprehend. Now that truly would be an Opera Obscura.

---

1 The Institute of Cybernetic Communication and Artificial Language. Based at the University of California, Berkeley, it continues to pursue its utopian vision of eliminating conflict by abolishing all existing languages and replacing them with an entirely new one, free from all organic prejudices.

2 Founded by Pierre Boulez and located in a bunker beneath the Pompidou Centre in Paris, the Institut de recherche et coordination acoustique/musique still attempts to do to music what the ICCAL intends for language.

x(0=z2x; <1000.0)<x=o/c2>

The main characters all had computer-generated names and sang from inside space suits. Samuel Ramey's voice was so powerful it broke the Perspex visor of his helmet on several occasions. Renée Fleming's character, <C3 =(Xy…100%)a-z>, can be seen in the Dalek-like costume. It was so hot and cramped that she lost nearly a stone in weight. Scenes like this have fuelled the frenzied speculation that the moon landings were all faked, or that NASA has had an operating base on the moon since the 1970s. It has even convinced many members of the Area 51 conspiracy community that the scene shows reverse-engineered alien spacecraft or an intergalactic peace conference on either Phobos or Deimos. Opinion remains divided, and IBM Bach cannot resolve matters. Like everything to do with Area 51, it is classified.

INCREDIBLE OPERA HOUSES

There are over 500 opera houses in the world – mainly in Europe, but North America has around sixty-five. They come in all sizes – from the gigantic Metropolitan in New York with 4,000 seats to the Teatro Antonio Belloni with ninety-eight.[1] The first opera houses were small, but in the nineteenth century opera became democratised and, as its audience grew, so did the size of its buildings. With lavish funds available, vast classical beaux-arts behemoths loomed in the world's major cities. Their bulk was necessary to contain the facilities to stage grand operas before large audiences.

The typical opera house seated about 1–2,000, arranged in a U-shaped auditorium, with boxes around the sides, stalls in the middle and vertiginous galleries above. Orchestra pits and stages were huge, and no opera house could be without the most ingenious stage machinery. Behind was a fly tower, into which the

---

[1] The Teatro Antonio Belloni is the smallest active opera house. The seventy-seat Vatican Opera House has been closed since the disastrous performance of *The Hammer of the Heretics* in 1912. (See p. 40.)

sets were hoisted by pulleys and counterweights. This meant a gigantic block dwarfing the auditorium, giving architects the difficult problem of incorporating its bulk in a harmonious composition.

The U-shaped form is the best acoustically and as a means to achieve an intimate relationship between the audience and stage. Modern departures from the format have rarely been successful and, apart from Sydney Opera House, none have won the hearts of the public who stubbornly prefer tuneful operas presented in auditoriums of gold and plush velvet. But, beside the large and impressive opera houses, there has always been room for the smaller, more intimate and eccentric. Glyndebourne and Snape started in very modest premises, and there will always be some lover of opera who dreams to turn an old cinema, a barn or even a caravan into their very own La Scala. The world is full of odd opera houses, and on the following pages are five of them, each unique and altogether extraordinary.

HMS SANS PAREIL

SIR PETER MAXWELL DAVIES often staged opera at the St Magnus Festival on Orkney, but it is now forgotten that there was once a floating opera house anchored in Scapa Flow. When the Grand Fleet moved to Scapa Flow in Orkney in 1914 at the outbreak of the First World War, the facilities for musical entertainments on-board ship soon proved inadequate. The Admiralty sent the old battleship HMS *Sans Pareil* to act as a floating theatre. The *Sans Pareil* was an obsolete ironclad, armed with two 16.25 inch guns mounted in a huge circular turret. This provided the base for the stage, which was divided into four sections, so rapid scene changes could be made by revolving the turret. Banks of seats were built up about the ship's bridge, and stage lighting was installed on a gantry fixed to the foremast.

It was not an entirely satisfactory arrangement. The seats, though roofed, were still open to icy blasts and the stage/turret revolved slowly, with much discordant grinding of gears. Patriotic opera singers journeyed to the far north to provide principals while the fleet furnished a large and stentorian chorus. From 1915 a series of productions was mounted: *Fringes of the Fleet* with words by Kipling and music by Elgar, Bizet's *The Pearl Fishers*, Ethel Smythe's *The Wreckers*, *Drake's Drum* by Henry Newbolt, with music by Arthur Goring Thomas, and *HMS Pinafore*, a constant favourite. Unfortunately the acoustics left much to be desired, and the *Sans Pareil* was soon dubbed *HMS Inaudible*, though some preferred the nickname *The Harmonious Battleship*.

In May 1916 a performance of Parry's *Moby Dick* was interrupted when the fleet was ordered to sea and, in the confusion, *Sans Pareil* received instructions to accompany the battleships. There was still some ammunition in the magazines, and the captain was eager to see action, but, by the time steam had been raised in the ancient boilers and the weed-entwined anchors raised, it was too late, and naval history was denied a unique chapter in which the world's greatest battle fleet went into action accompanied by its own opera house. After the armistice *Sans Pareil* staged her last production – *The Flying Dutchman* – with an audience from the interned German High Seas Fleet. Then the curtain came down for the last time, and the world's only floating ironclad opera house was towed away to Faslane to be scrapped.

The vast extent of the Scapa Flow anchorage meant that the waters could at times be almost as rough as the open sea. The only time the cast of *HMS Pinafore* have ever been actually seasick was at a performance given during a gale in 1917. In 1918 the crew of the visiting Japanese battlecruiser *Kongo* gave a performance of *Closer to the Enemy* (see p. 34), which was politely received. Admiral Jellicoe's Flag-Commander, The Hon. Reginald A.R. Plunkett, a keen ornithologist, spent most of his time off duty attempting to train a chorus of seagulls and skuas, but with limited success.

THE TIN DUNNY AT WOMBAWOMBA

Corrugated iron could have been invented just for Australia: in a land where labour and good building timber were scarce, it was the ideal material for buildings that needed to be erected quickly. Manufacturers in England produced an extensive range of prefabricated corrugated iron buildings, including cottages, public houses, ballrooms,[1] railway stations, churches and agricultural buildings of every description. By the 1850s whole towns were being shipped out to Australia in packing cases to be carted into the bush and assembled.

The chief customers for corrugated iron buildings were the sheep stations in the outback, which by the 1880s were vast in extent and generating great wealth. The largest of all was WombaWomba in South Australia, which was twice as big as Yorkshire. The empress of this realm of sheep was the hard-riding and soft-spoken Frederica Dedstock. She returned from her sole visit to Europe with a passion for opera and, as the nearest theatre was 600 miles away in Adelaide, decided to build her own. There was nothing suitable in the catalogues of any of the corrugated-iron manufacturers, so she commissioned Samuel Hemmings of Bristol to build an opera house to her own specifications. They obliged by combining their second-class colonial legislature chamber with the tropical Roman Catholic basilica (campanile optional).

The opera house arrived at WombaWomba in 127 packing cases, accompanied by thirteen artisans to erect it. There was seating for 150, with two private boxes lined with red plush, a fifty-foot fly tower and a revolving stage. It was built within a month, and, although given the grandiose name of Teatro Australis, was always known as the 'Tin Dunny'. In July 1881 an exhausted Carl Rosa opera company arrived after a ninety-mile trek in bullock carts to give a performance of Mayerbeer's *The Hugenots*.

Subsequent performances were infrequent, few artists being willing to make the long journey into the outback. One who did was the young Nellie Melba, who gave a concert of *Lieder* in 1884, shortly after her Melbourne debut, but, by the 1890s, most performances were given by the sheep station's amateur company assembled from the servants, stockmen and itinerant shearers. One of the best tenors was the notorious bushranger Ukulele Harrison, but he was rarely available. The opera house was probably not best suited for these rough-and-ready performances, as the acoustics were bad, it was insufferably hot, the iron creaked and groaned as it expanded and contracted and, on the rare occasions when it rained, the impromptu percussion was overwhelming.[2]

After Frederica's death in 1910, her son Gordon, who had no interest in music (or sheep), converted the opera house into a shooting range and roller-skating rink, which remained until 1947 when it was turned into a shearing shed, which still survives.

---

1 Prince Albert bought one and had it erected at Balmoral.
2 The sound of rain falling on corrugated iron was the soundtrack to much of Australian life and was celebrated in the seven-minute-long *Tin Symphony* played at the closing ceremony of the Sydney Olympics.

THE TIN DUNNY AT WOMBAWOMBA

There were plans by Heritage South Australia to restore the WombaWomba opera house to its former glory in time for a revival of *The Fatal Compact* (see p. 58) in the centenary year of Banjo McKenzie's birth, but these came to nothing, as did a proposed fundraising concert by Nick Cave and the Bad Seeds. In 2020 the Tin Dunny narrowly escaped being destroyed by an enormous bush fire.

DOM SOLNY

THE ONLY UNDERGROUND OPERA HOUSE in the world lies almost a thousand feet (three hundred metres) under fields outside the Polish city of Kraków. Salt has been mined there since the twelfth century, creating an underworld of mystery and strange beauty. Worked-out parts of the mine were adapted to provide accommodation, including taverns, chapels and even a ballroom. The miners had a strong musical tradition, and each gang had its own work song which they sang as they marched to work.[1]

In 1720 several caverns were enlarged to form the world's first and only underground opera house. With elaborate baroque decoration, Dom Solny (The Salt House) was as sumptuous as any theatre in Italy or Germany. The stage machinery was ingenious and elaborate, the acoustics exceptional, although the dry atmosphere sometimes affected the singers' voices.

Throughout the eighteenth century works by all the leading composers were performed there. In the nineteenth century both Liszt and Chopin played upon the subterranean stage and Jenny Lind sang. Wagner, when exiled and penniless, composed and conducted a chorus for the miners' annual singing gala, and the experience influenced his conception of the Nibelungens in the Ring Cycle.

In the twentieth century, because of the small size of the opera house (only 600 seats), and its inconvenience outweighing its charm, hardly any musical performances were staged, and there was talk of converting it into a cinema. During the Second World War, under German occupation, opera was revived under the patronage of the music-loving Gauleiter Heinrich Koch, with a performance of the ever popular *Der Fliegende Hamburger* (see p. 48). After Koch's assassination by partisans in 1943, Dom Solny was converted into a factory to make components for the V5.[2]

Restored and renovated in the 1950s, Dom Solny is now a UNESCO World Heritage Site, and is an appropriate venue for the biannual Festival of Avant Garde and Underground Music. In 2013 the first, and only, Polish rap opera, Jan Popowynszki's *Paktofonika*, was premiered there. An appropriate location, as the work has never emerged into the light of day.

---

1 The miners wore a tunic with a pointed hood and this uniform, combined with their subterranean singing, is surely the inspiration for the dwarves in Snow White.
2 The V5, of which no trace has ever been found, is said to have been a flying saucer powered by antigravity. Some of the aviation conspiracy community believe that the United States has the prototype at Area 51 in Nevada, but others assert that a whole squadron was built which flew Hitler, Martin Bormann and other top Nazis to a remote location in the Andes, where they still make occasional flights connected with the cocaine trade.

Dom Solny has now been restored to its former glory. The front-of-house staff and stagehands wear medieval miners' tunics and hoods. Not all are happy about this.

THE AERIAL OPERA HOUSE NO 1

IT WAS LIKE A COLLABORATION between Wagner and H.G. Wells: an enormous airship containing an opera house roaming across the United States, bringing culture to every remote community. Such was the dream of Cecil B. DeMille and J.P. Morgan, who founded the Transcontinental Peripatetic Opera Company in 1929. They approached the industrial designer Norman Bel Geddes and commissioned him to design a flying opera house. Bel Geddes' influence was enormous, and much of the look of the modern world, particularly in the 1930s and 1940s, with its absence of colour, insistence on natural light, simple lines and ubiquitous streamlining, can be laid at the door of his office on 9th Avenue, New York.[1]

He eagerly accepted the commission, and proposed reworking his gargantuan seaplane, *Aircraft No 4*, until it was pointed out that most of the places with lakes and rivers wide enough for it to land already had opera houses. Undaunted, Bel Geddes went back to the drawing board,[2] and designed *Aerial Opera House No 1* – a giant airship with an auditorium that would seat 750. It was not intended that performances would take place while the airship was flying at high altitude. Instead it would hover over a town and winch up its audience in baskets. Constructed from aluminium, light spruce and papier mâché, the weight was kept down to 250 tons. Allowing for fifty tons of audience, orchestra and cast, this meant a total weight of 300 tons. It required an airship with a capacity of 14 million cubic feet of hydrogen contained in an envelope 900 feet long by 180 feet in diameter. This was gigantic – twice as big as the German zeppelin *Hindenburg*.

Work began on the auditorium, which was completed in 1930 and several frames of the giant gas bag were erected. The first production was already booked[3] and programmes printed when the worsening financial situation – as well as technical problems caused by the need to increase engine power to overcome the drag of the auditorium – loomed. Critics pointed out that although Bel Geddes streamlined everything that did not move, he had neglected to streamline the one thing that did. The decision to dispense with the orchestra and replace them with gramophones was the final blow to the project, and it was cancelled in 1931.[4] The auditorium was displayed at the World's Fair in New York in 1964, where it still survives, although converted to an IMAX cinema.

---

1 Geddes had previously designed sets for DeMille's Hollywood epic films.
2 He designed it himself, of course. It is still in production.
3 *La Fanciulla del West* by Puccini, starring Rosa Ponselle as Minnie and Beniamino Gigli as Dick Johnson.
4 Bel Geddes' connection with opera continued after his death when his daughter, Barbara, starred in the soap opera *Dallas*.

An optimistic rendition of the giant airship and opera house bringing much-needed culture to a small town in Kansas. It was intended to fit loudspeakers to the airship so that those on the ground could share the performance. Tests with a captive balloon over Des Moines were inconclusive. Thirty per cent liked music from the sky, forty-five per cent disapproved, twenty per cent had no opinion and five per cent thought they were going mad.

THE ARCHIGRAM OPERA HOUSE

THERE ARE OPERA LOVERS in the most far-flung places who will go to the most extraordinary lengths to attend performances or arrange for opera companies to come to them. The group of Fijians who canoed 1,700 miles to the Royal Whanganui Opera House in New Zealand to attend a performance of *The Pearl Fishers* are only outdone by the Inuit who sledged 1,800 miles from Hudson Bay to Toronto's Grand Opera House to hear *Tosca*.

The nitrate miners on Chile's long northern coastline were of Italian extraction, and their national love of opera was only increased by the bleak landscape of their exile – *Nabucco* was an obvious favourite. Humperdinck's *Hansel and Gretel*, Weber's *The Forest Maiden* and Wagner's *Siegfried* were also very popular, as much for the trees as the music.

The only way to reach the isolated settlements on the fringe of the Atacama Desert was by sea. However, whether the opera companies could land depended on the state of the surf. Often it was so high it was impossible to reach the shore, and many an eagerly awaited performance had to be cancelled – ironically *The Flying Dutchman* was particularly cursed by the waves.

An ingenious solution to the problem was found in the 1960s, when the world's only mobile opera house was constructed, capable of moving up and down the 600 miles of arid coastline. The Chilean Miners' Union commissioned British architect Ron Herron to build them a Walking Opera House. Herron, and the visionary group of architects known as Archigram, had developed the concept of the Walking City, a metropolis that could move on enormous telescopic steel legs. Herron adapted this to create a travelling auditorium that would carry a complete opera company up and down the coast.

The election of the left-wing government of Salvador Allende in 1970 resulted in funds being made available, and work began immediately. Many of Herron's original ideas proved either technically unfeasible or staggeringly expensive, so compromises had to be made. The Archigram Opera House was unveiled in August 1973.

The first production was to be *Hijas desencadenadas* (Daughters Unchained) by the radical Marxist and feminist Vita Vivado.[1] On the 9th of September 1973 the great diesel engines of the Archigram Opera House thundered into life and it began to rumble towards Tocopilla for the first performance. Progress was slow and steering erratic. There were widespread blackouts as power lines were torn down and several cottages, a garage and a cemetery chapel were ground to rubble beneath the opera house's gigantic tracks. Tocopilla was never reached.

On the 11th of September a military junta launched a coup and overthrew President Allende. The Archigram Opera House was targeted by the Chilean Air Force, and was struck by several rockets and a large bomb. The attack was specifically ordered by General Pinochet, whose tastes in architecture and music were as conservative as his politics.

---

1 The selection of the first opera caused a split in the Miners' Union. The conservative majority wanted *Nabucco*, but branch meetings were packed with radicals who made sure Vivado's work was chosen.

THE ARCHIGRAM OPERA HOUSE

The main component of the mobile opera house was the base unit of a 1,500-ton mobile dragline excavator. On top of this were fitted a fly tower (using an old nitrate silo), a stage and an auditorium (constructed from a redundant gasometer). Maximum audience capacity was 500, and top speed was two miles per hour. The rusting remains of the world's only mobile opera house can still be found a few miles from Tocopilla, between the Ruta 1 highway and the beach. Increasingly popular with adventurous tourists, they have been featured on the Yesterday Channel's *Abandoned Engineering* and in a Gucci fashion shoot. Safety concerns regarding unexploded ordnance prevented them being used as a location for scenes in the 2008 Bond film *The Quantum of Solace*.

INCREDIBLE INSTRUMENTS

U P TO THE MID-NINETEENTH CENTURY composers wrote operas for the available orchestra and its limited variety of instruments, but after about 1850 they could muster much larger and more varied musical forces. The century's mechanical ingenuity provided them with many novel instruments. Wagner invented the Wagner tuba – a cross between the French Horn and a tuba – Adolphe Sax and John Sousa provided their eponymous 'phones', and there were all kinds of weird contraptions where ingenuity trumped musical sense. The gigantic Octobass needed a system of levers and clamps to play, for the thickness of its strings and the length of its fingerboard was beyond the strength of any musician's hand. From the 1830s the power of steam was utilised to more or less tuneful effect in the steam organ, although this does not seem to have been used in any operas. As well as all these complex instruments, there is always room in the orchestra pit for the simple – particularly in the percussion section: teacups, cutlery and washboards have all made their contribution. In the twentieth century electronics produced an even greater variety of sounds, beginning with the invention of the Ondes Martenot, and continues through the use of synthesisers, samplers and computers. Whether these electronic noises are worth the trouble is debatable.

CALLIOPE
Named after the Greek muse, the Calliope is a steam organ invented in 1855. It is not a subtle instrument (there is no way to vary tone or volume), which was why it was used in *The Empty Casserole*.

COWBELLS
In orchestral and operatic music the sound of bells is mostly created by tubular bells, composers have often used handbells or carillons, which are operated by a keyboard. These Swiss cowbells were used in *The Frayed Rope*.

DIDGERIDOO
The traditional instruments of Australian aborigines, the didgeridoo is the only woodwind instrument made by ants – traditionally, they are bored out by termites. Varying in length from three to ten feet, they produce a musical drone. The only opera in which one has been featured is *The Fatal Compact*.

THEREMIN
Invented by a Russian scientist in 1919, the theremin was one of the first electronic instruments, and came to be the soundtrack of science fiction. It is capable of weird, unearthly sounds, which are produced by oscillators modified by the position of the player's hands in relation to the protruding antennae. It figured prominently in *Reach for the Stars*.

ONDES MARTENOT

Named after its inventor, Maurice Martenot, the Ondes Martenot was invented in 1928. Easier to play than the theremin, as it has a five-octave keyboard, it produces similar eerie, haunting sounds. The only operas scored for it are Thomas Adès' *Exterminating Angel* and Oresund's *Are We There Yet?*

TUNED CAR SPRING

The great percussionist James Blades adapted the rear spring of a Rolls Royce to produce a harmonious clang as an anvil for Benjamin Britten's *The Burning Fiery Furnace*. It was struck by a bolt.

CRYSTALLOPHONE

A nineteenth-century innovation based on an age-old concept, the crystallaphone was very popular in North and South America. It consists of glasses that are carefully arranged and either rubbed with wet hands or struck with small hammers. The glasses used in *The Golden Bean of Death* were charged with champagne.

YUNLUO

Between ten and forty small bronze gongs are suspended in a frame to make this very popular instrument in Chinese classical music. A great frame of twenty-four gongs, each seven *chi* (eight feet) in diameter, was created as part of the orchestra for the initial production of *The Emperor's Harmonious and Heavenly Fist*.

VEENA

Very similar in design to the sitar, with a horizontal fingerboard stretched between two gourd resonators. Its only appearance in European opera was in *Count Your Blessings*.

WIND MACHINE

The wind machine is played by rotating the crank handle to create friction between the wooden slats and the material covering that touches the cylinder, thus producing the sound of rushing wind. Rossini, Ravel, Puccini and Wagner all made use of it, as did Vaughan Williams in *Opera Antarctica*.

ANVIL

Although Wagner scored *Das Rheingold* for eighteen tuned anvils, they had to be specially made, as real blacksmiths' anvils do not vibrate harmonically. Most composers make do with lengths of tuned steel or car springs.

OPHICLEIDE

The name means 'keyed serpent', though it was often mocked as the 'chromatic bullock'. This giant early tuba was introduced in the early nineteenth century. It was first scored for opera in Spontini's *Olimpie*, and made one of its last appearances in *The Lucky Card*.

OCTOBASS

The octobass was tuned an octave lower than the modern double bass. It was twelve feet high and usually required two players. The three strings were so thick they could only be held down by a system of clamps. Loved by Berlioz, six were used in *The Empty Casserole*. When all played their lowest G together the Eiffel Tower vibrated.

CANNON

Only at an outdoor performance of the 1812 Overture is it possible to have real gunfire. In the modern day blanks can be used for indoor performances. In *Closer to the Enemy* the sound of cannons was created by firing revolvers into a drum filled with sand.

ALPHORN

Imitated by conventional instruments in Beethoven's *Pastoral Symphony*, tuned alphorns were later used in ensemble performances. Although many composers used alphorn motifs, only Strauss in *Daphne* and Raff in *The Frayed Rope* actually scored the alphorn for an opera.

LOCOMOTIVE WHISTLE

American locomotive manufacturers in the nineteenth century vied with each other to produce tuneful whistles for the railroads. Only two sounds habitually broke the profound silence of the empty prairie: the howl of a lonesome coyote and a jolly rendering of some popular song from the whistle of a passing locomotive. A whistle from an old Union Pacific locomotive featured prominently in the *Long, Long Train o' Misery*, although transposed to a melancholy D minor.

A SELECTIVE GLOSSARY

ARIA: A song which must have a hummable tune and some vocal fireworks to allow the prima donna and tenor to show off. An opera without a single memorable aria might please the critics but nobody else.

BARITONE: The male voice between tenor and bass. Frequently a doting father or a villain who tries to thwart the tenor of his rightful romantic prize.

BASS: The lowest male voice, suitable for wise or wicked men, but never the romantic hero. Russian operas have a lot of them, with long beards and heavy robes.

CASTRATO: A man who has been surgically altered to preserve his unbroken voice. Haydn narrowly escaped this procedure, which was not banned in Italy until 1870.

CONTRALTO: The deepest female voice. Ideal for queens, sibyls and other very important women who are not meant to be considered attractive. Never gets the tenor.

CHORUS: A group of singers who back the principals while dreaming of replacing them.

COSTUMES: Sometimes spectacular and often silly. The one essential requirement, often ignored by designers, is not to hinder the singer's mobility or breathing. (Think corsets and very high heels. And hats with spinning plates!)

COUNTERTENORS: Are not tenors at all, but high altos. Alfred Deller was the first modern countertenor, and was always having to explain that he was 'unique', not a 'eunuch'.

DIVA: See Prima Donna.

INTERVAL: A fairly long period between acts for set-changing, breath-catching, ice-cream-eating, bar-propping and small talk. Some people's favourite bit.

LEITMOTIF: A short musical phrase linked to an idea, object or character that conveniently nudges the audience at appropriate moments. Wagner was very keen on them, as are composers of film scores. Wagnerites are obsessed with them.

LIBRETTO: Both words to the sung parts and any spoken passages. Since the music provides the tone and emotion, the words themselves are quite often mundane. There is much repetition. A little can go a very long way. A frequent cause of tension between composer and writer. The worst libretti are usually written by the composer. Except Wagner.

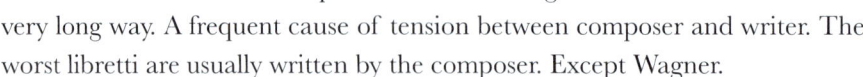

OPERA: Literally 'the work'; the combination of music and drama. The original simple form has evolved into many varieties. Such as…

1. BALLAD OPERA: Light, often farcical English opera with simple themes and music. Its other main virtue is that it is tuneful.

2. OPERA BUFFA: Opera with a comic subject and usually with spoken dialogue. It is derived from commedia dell'arte – but do not hold that against it, as it is often genuinely funny.

3. OPÉRA COMIQUE: The French term for opera with spoken dialogue. Not to be confused with comic opera, which is meant to be funny, opéra comique can be tragic.

4. GRAND OPERA: Opera without spoken dialogue. It does not necessarily need an epic plot, enormous cast, overpowering music, sumptuous costumes and spectacular sets but, as 'grand' creates expectations of scale, audiences are disappointed if it does not.

5. MODERN OPERA: Generally turns its back on all the qualities that made opera popular. But who needs melody and harmony when there is subsidy?

6. OPERA SERIA: Literally, Serious Opera. Popular in the early eighteenth century, when audiences were thrilled by interminable works on tragic classical themes with the male lead sung by a castrato.

7. OPERETTA: Light and tuneful romantic nineteenth century opera with spoken dialogue. The best ones are French, which are risqué in a moustache-tweaking, petticoat-swishing way. They have evolved into the modern musical.

A SELECTIVE GLOSSARY

8. ORATORIO: A sacred opera without action and with limited visual effects. Most have a single eponymous title, like an airport novel: *Saul*, *Elijah*, *Daniel*, *Esther*. They were once very popular with thrifty northern choral societies. (The money they saved on sets could be spent on a conductor like Sir Malcolm Sargent.)

9. ZEITOPER: Literally, 'opera of its time', a genre of the 1920s and 30s with a contemporary theme employing modern inventions like telephones, typewriters, trains and electric toasters. Peenemunde's *Der Fliegende Hamburger* was once the most famous example, although the support of its infamous fans has now consigned it to oblivion.

OVERTURE: The opening piece. It often begins very loudly to still the chattering audience, and usually introduces the main themes. Some do this so successfully that one needs never to listen to the whole opera again; everyone knows von Suppe's *Light Cavalry* overture, but the rest is silence.

PRIMA DONNA: A soprano of thrilling voice and volcanic temperament. In the 1950s they filled the gossip columns and married millionaires and minor royalty.

SETS: Basically a flat screen painted either in scrupulous realism or abstract abandon. In the nineteenth century, with the perfection of stage machinery, sets became needlessly elaborate. Castles, pyramids, railway trains and the River Rhine all appeared on stage. Since the 1950s the fashion has been for symbolic minimalism, but budgets do not seem to have been drastically reduced. In this case, less often does mean more.

SOPRANO: The heroine who wins the hero and the audience's adulation with her thrilling top notes, which sometimes shatter champagne glasses. Sopranos used to be rather bulky, hence the idiom, and while this is no longer usually the case there has been no discernible reduction in vocal power. An opera without a showpiece for the voice of its leading lady is… modern.

TENOR: The male star, who always gets the girl, usually only after seeing off the baritone. Most tenors project their egos as powerfully as their voices. On occasions they have married Prima Donnas, to the delight of the gossip columns.

ZINGARA, À LA: Sung in a gypsy style. An eighteenth and nineteenth century way to appear more edgy and earthy. An early way of getting street cred.